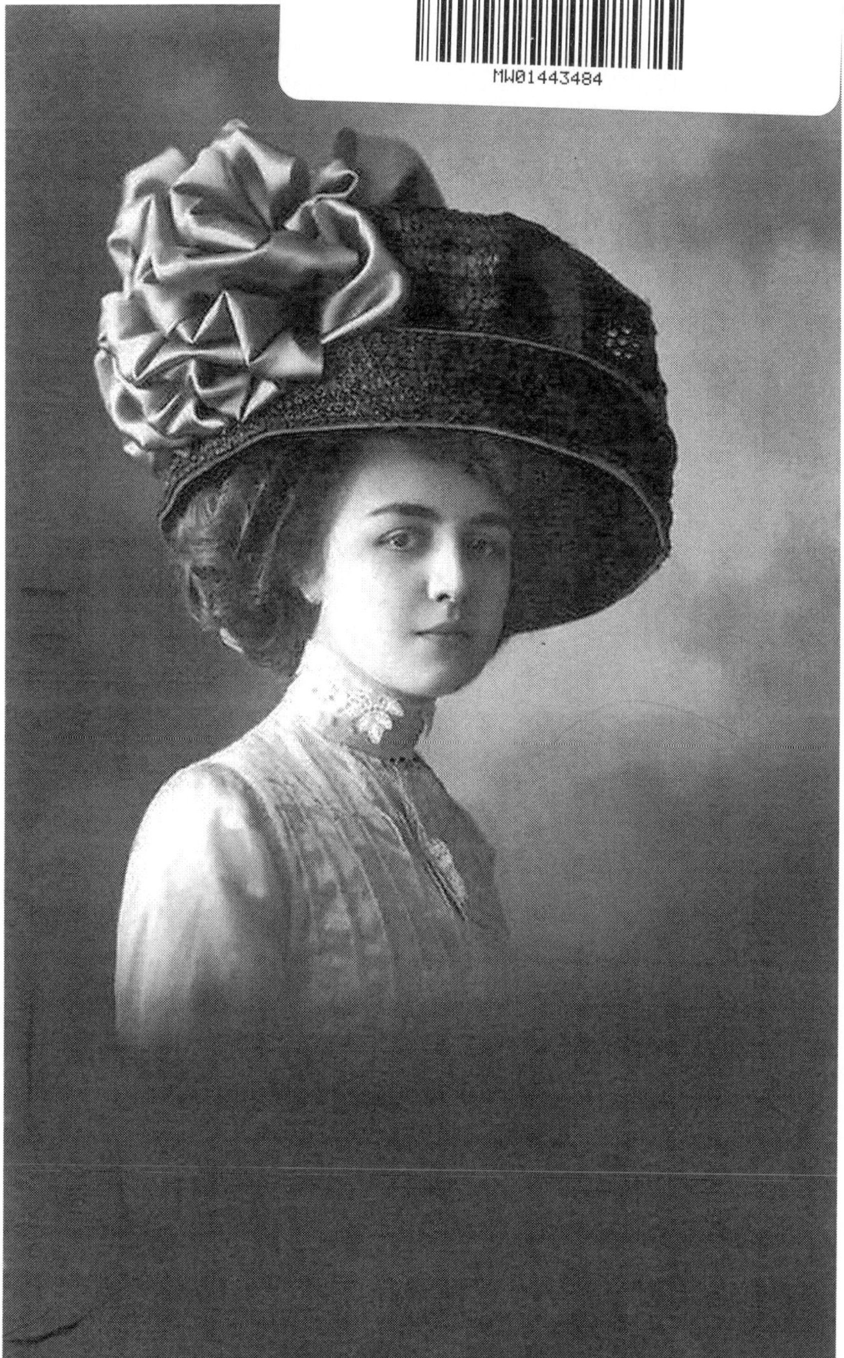

Stories by Stephen Carey Fox

The End of Illusion
The German, 'Mr. Kai' and The Devil
Artists, Thieves & Liars
The Collector
Lou & Billy Joe
The Ghost of Yesterdays
Blame Jason Bourne
Everybody Knew ... Nobody Knew
The Elephant in the Room
The Robin Hood Solution

Stephen Carey Fox

A MOST IMPROBABLE UNION

The DAR

& the Coal Man

A Most Improbable Union
The DAR & the Coal Man

This is a work of fiction. Names, characters, businesses, places, events, and incidents are either the product of the author's imagination or used in a fictitious manner. In some instances, resemblance to persons and actual events is neither imaginary nor fictitious.

'The Hottest Stuff in Town' from the
Album Rare Jazz and Blues Piano (1927–1937)

Cover: Courtesy of opheliarowan.tumbir.com

ISBN: 979-8388800671

Copyright © 2021 Stephen Carey Fox
& Mickeysgod Publications
All rights reserved.

www.mickeysgod.info

Precis		7
Part I	*Newcomers*	8
Part II	*Flowering*	38
Part III	*Ardor*	72
Part IV	*Altered States*	132
Part V	*Trials*	158
Part VI	*Siblings*	182
Part VII	*Reminiscence*	200
Part VIII	*Second-Class Citizens*	222
Part IX	*Swansong*	276
Part X	*Afterword*	296
Debts		303
Author		305

PRECIS

This story follows the lives of two people, polar opposites, drawn together at the dawn of the 20th century: one from western New York and the other from Germany; one a Daughter of the American Revolution, the other an immigrant coal man.

Carolyn, the daughter of a wealthy manufacturer, knew little else than the secure world of conservative economic, political and social values.

Conrad, the second son of a village shoemaker, knew nothing of Carolyn's world. His ancestors, ground down by perpetual poverty, the pawns of endless European wars and resultant migrations, couldn't possibly have been the 'sons' or 'daughters' of anything so grand as a revolution.

Those who knew the pair scratched their heads in amazement at their improbable union ...

PART I
NEWCOMERS

1 *BELGENLAND*

Anna Maria Bauer extended her arms toward the boy. One hand clutched a bowl from which a spoon threatened to topple as the S.S. *Belgenland* corkscrewed through the North Atlantic swells, its steel-plated sides groaning in protest.

Those moans became a chorus of misery when echoed by the steerage passengers, as though the two, flesh and steel, were one. Occasionally, the *Belgenland* topped swells tall enough to lift the propellers clear of the water as it pitched toward the bottom of the trough, vibrating the entire vessel as though God had reached down and given it a warning shake.

"*Kommen her*, Konrad. *Setz dich neben mich*," Anna Maria pleaded to the boy, who sat on the deck, pale and terribly seasick, his rump and back against the cold, damp bulkhead.

"Don't be frightened. I can warm you. It's time you ate something, even if it's only soup. I know there isn't much, but if you can, you should."

He was too miserable to nod or shake his head.

The boy's mother and his two sisters sat ten feet away. They and a handful of other steerage passengers occupied the top of a box of life preservers.

Marta, 12, and Louise Bauer, 15, used both hands and their laps to steady their bowls. Normal dining facilities—tables and chairs—for open-berth steerage passengers were inadequate or non-existent, which forced them to compete for a place atop the box. The typical excuse offered by the company in defense of such a stingy policy was that 'immigrants are not used to tables and chairs and do not miss them when they are lacking.'

The women struggled continuously to keep the thin broth within their bowls as the steamer pitched and rolled toward the immigration station at Castle Garden and New York City.

§

Eleven-year-old Konrad Bauer, who had managed to keep down only two spoonful's of soup, lay shivering under two blankets his mother had taken surreptitiously from the berths of the dead. Konrad's body, grown scrawny from lack of nourishment, produced little heat. Each time the *Belgenland* pitched, which in the North Atlantic happened with unnerving regularity every few seconds, or when he turned his head, his body heaved in another empty retch.

Konrad's misery, familiar to anyone who has been seasick, began for him and hundreds of other steerage passengers the moment their ship left Holland's Scheldt estuary and entered the North Sea and English Channel. Konrad Bauer desperately wanted that ship to turn around and return him to dry land—anywhere. America had never been his idea anyway. Steerage meant something quite different to Konrad than it did to his mother and doubtless his sisters, as well.

What must an eleven-year-old boy have been thinking? He would never live to see his twelfth birthday. He didn't care about soup, his mother, or his sisters. That he ever left Bierstadt. Whether he lived or died. Perhaps least of all, whether he ever saw America. And why not? Who could imagine such a place? Certainly not him, his mother, his sisters, or any of the hundreds of steerage and cabin passengers.

The smell of wet coal smoke filled his nostrils. The vibration of the deck and bulkhead where he tried to sleep kept him awake. He couldn't warm himself no matter how many blankets his mother piled on. He hadn't the strength to relieve himself in the public troughs intended for that purpose. So, day and night—he never knew which it was—he lay in clothes dampened by urine and fouled by excrement.

No, he just wanted everyone to leave him alone to die. He especially wanted no more of his mother's earnestness, her explanations of why they must go to America, or her constant, cheerful chatter about a 'new life.' He prayed night and day the ship might sink. That would show them how wrong they were!

§

One doesn't dare to think of what those thousands of men, women and children experienced in the dark, stifling belly of ocean liners, living amid starvation, disease, and death. It is easy, perhaps, to understand that many such passengers and sympathetic outsiders saw the 'new' ocean liners as simply a fresh generation of slave ships. But Anna Maria Bauer would have none of that! Despite her own and her son's misery—even that of her daughters' who thankfully never spoke of it—she could never have thought of the *Belgenland* as a slave ship. To her, the ship spoke only of a new life, a life of mystery and excitement, not of misery and imprisonment. She was free to fly!

Slave ships or no, when the Bauers put to sea in the early 1880s, there was a greater risk of dying by staying in Europe than by emigrating to America. To make that risk even more palatable, the steamship companies lowered the average passage to nearly that of a month's unskilled wages in the United States.

These enticements had little influence on Anna Maria's decision to leave Germany. Her husband of twenty-two years, Georg Bauer, a shoemaker in the Baden-Württemberg village of Bierstadt, had died of consumption, leaving the family without means of support and little choice other than to begin life anew elsewhere.

Doubtless, some macro events or trends—poor climate conditions that lowered crop yields and market prices, political upheavals, war—influenced their decision in immeasurable ways. A factor that one could measure stood out. Otto von Bismarck had created a powerful, well-equipped military, and in the space of a decade, he led Prussia into three wars that paved the way for German unity. Anna Maria Bauer, who cared nothing for German unity, had two sons she did care for and did not wish to sacrifice to the ambitions of a strutting Prussian.

In the end, the most obvious of motives drove her family from Teningen to the New World: the Bauers had no sustained financial support without Georg.

§

> *The New York Times*, September 19, 1882—
> For many fleeing Europe, low fares allowed even the poorest of the poor to book passage on an Atlantic steamship as 'steerage' passengers ('steerage' refers to the inner bowels of a ship where the crew stored steering equipment—rudders and so forth). But if any migrants thought they were getting a bargain for the low price, perhaps they should have paid attention to what other travelers had to say of their experiences. A 'bargain' is seldom a bargain.
> Accommodations, some said, ranged from fair to atrocious, the food from tasty to inedible, the crews from helpful to brutish. The pitch and roll of the ship tossed passengers from their berths. During storms, the captain ordered

steerage passengers below decks for days at a time, without access to toilets, natural light, or fresh air. Others described unbearable air, 'miserable' food and violations of privacy amongst passengers 'packed like cattle' in a travel class 'unfit for human beings.' And females endured other forms of degradation dished out by crewmen, whose language and conversation were vile, their comments about women uncouth.

Contrarians reported shipboard service 'far above expectation,' their days filled with 'fun.' Voyages were 'smooth and pleasant' with hours of dancing, amusement, and unmatched fellowship.

In time, particularly after 1855, came reform. The White Star Line, for example, allowed families to stay together in individual cabins and guaranteed separate berths for each adult steerage passenger, along with a baggage allowance. Children could travel for half price, and passengers had to be medically healthy, preventing any more outbreaks of disease onboard. A steerage ticket guaranteed three cooked meals a day. To millions of impoverished and slum-dwelling urban workers, such conditions seemed luxurious.

No matter what others thought of the experience, good or bad, or if legislation could improve the appalling conditions, it meant nothing to Konrad Bauer. But his mother never gave up trying to make it meaningful. She may have sensed her son's misery, but she never allowed him to know that she understood or would tolerate it. In that lay defeat. Instead, her mind fixated, as it should have, on assuring that what remained of her family made it safely to America.

"You must try to put aside how miserable you feel, Konrad. This voyage is a glimmer of hope for us, a chance for a new life ..."

'There it was again,' he seethed, 'that infernal 'new life' of hers!' He wanted to stuff her mouth with cloths to shut her up.

"When your father died there was nothing left for us in Bierstadt. I've explained that to you many times. So, we are going to Pieter in the state of North Dakota—and we will be there soon!"

§

Pieter, twenty-one, was the oldest of Georg and Anna Maria's four children. While a young boy, he had learned the shoemaking trade at his father's elbow. Two years earlier, before the rest of his family found themselves aboard the *Belgenland*, he had set forth for the New World and established himself as a shoemaker in Griggs, a small place, not yet incorporated as a town, a circumstance the railroad would change forever. Pieter felt comfortable there. Those of German descent (41 percent) already made up nearly half the town's population. Add to that the Norwegians at 32 percent, and you have three-quarters of the inhabitants.

§

Konrad thought for a moment about his older brother who he adored. His mother's intentional mention of Pieter seemed to have done the trick, creating a momentary spark of life in the despondent little boy.

In moments of lucidity, when he wasn't so cold and he'd tolerated some soup and dried pork, he would momentarily forget her 'new life' and say, "Do you promise, *Mutti*? That we'll be there soon?"

"Yes, of course. Now, I want you to stop feeling sorry for yourself. Everyone here is miserable, but you don't hear them complain, do you?"

Defeated, Konrad looked around, but to his eye no one, not a single soul, looked as pitiable as he felt. He'd already forgotten Pieter.

"No, *Mutti*."

2   TO GRAND CENTRAL

Pieter Bauer stepped ashore at Castle Garden in 1879 into a world he couldn't have imagined in tiny Bierstadt, Baden-Württemberg. Crowds of busy, purposeful people moved at lightning speed, in and out of the tallest buildings he had ever seen. The towering giants hovered above the streets, seemingly about to tip over. As he walked, he felt he was passing from one cave into another.

    Other sights and impressions offered striking contrasts. Elegant brownstone buildings stood next to houses made of wood and scrap metal. Streets of cobblestone melted into streets of dirt. Mud and manure everywhere.

Housing in the southern tip of Manhattan, which included Castle Garden, bulged with newly built wooden tenements and behind them, flimsy wooden shacks. Italians settled around Mulberry Street between the East Village and Lower Manhattan, later known as 'Little Italy.' Yiddish-speaking Eastern European Jews called the Lower East Side home.

Pieter Bauer couldn't possibly have ignored an even more striking phenomenon: noxious odors. He smelled them at once. They seemed slightly familiar, but this was a huge city, not a rural backwater, and he couldn't place all of them. As he exited the Castle Garden station, he stopped the exit gate to ask a question of the uniformed man in black, who he took to be a guard.

"Excuse me, sir," he said in his best but rough-cut English. "I'm new here, and I'm curious about that strong odor. Do you know what it is?"

Now, Pieter had seen the horse dung on the streets, so his query bordered at best on the naïve and at worst on the disingenuous. Without realizing it, he had invited disrespect.

The guard began to laugh.

"*Sind Sie Deutscher? Oder Norwegsich?* the man mocked."

"Yes, *Deutscher.*"

"Well, son, since you come from a shitty country, you should recognize that smell."

"Excuse me, what do you mean by a 'shitty' country?"

To demonstrate the guard squeezed his nose. "Now move along!"

"Not before you explain that smell. I asked you respectfully. I didn't disrespect your country, which I plan to make my home. I'm free to do that here, aren't I?"

The man thought better of an argument over 'freedom,' plus he saw his supervisor approaching.

"If I tell you about that smell, will you move along?"

"Before you can say Frederick the Great!"

"Is there a problem here, Bert?" the supervisor asked.

"No sir. This fine young gentleman was just inquiring about the smell."

"And you explained it to him?"

"Ready to do just that, Chief."

"Thank you, Bert," he said dismissively. "By the way, did you welcome this fine young man to New York and America?" He didn't wait for the guard to answer. "Where are you from, son?"

"Germany."

"Oh, I see. Lots of you folks just disembarked, right?"

"Yes, sir."

"Well, if Bert didn't say it, I will. Welcome to the greatest city in the world. Enjoy your stay. Oh, by the way, where're you headed?"

"Dakota, sir."

"What's your trade?"

Pieter hesitated, unsure of the word 'trade.' The chief should have known.

"What is your work?"

"Yes! ... Shoemaker."

"Well, I'm sure there's plenty of need for shoes out there in Dakota Territory. Best of luck."

The chief wandered off, but before he left the pair, he told the guard to check with the personnel office at the end of his shift.

Pieter understood enough English, facial expressions, and body language to realize the rude guard might be on his way out. He turned to continue their conversation.

"You were about to explain that awful smell."

The man's attitude toward Pieter had changed sharply. That impressed Pieter, and he wondered if the chief might not be German! He had known school masters with that same manner of setting things straight.

"Oh, yeah," the man said. The chief's 'visit' had clearly shaken him. "Forgot. It's simple, really. Dead horses and manure."

"What?"

"You heard me. Dead horses and manure. You see, we got about 170,000 of those beasts used for transportation. Likely you'll soon see for yourself. That adds up to about 3–4 million pounds of shit every day, figuring each pony grunts out 15–30 pounds. The streetcar drivers don't treat 'em well, so, many just die on right there on the street, still in their harness and trace. Fifteen thousand every year!"

"Then what happens to them? Wouldn't they be hard to move?"

"Sure are. Need special wagons. A horse weighs near a ton and a half."

"'Ton and a half'? In pounds?" Pieter looked down, trying to convert pounds to metrics.

"You bet. A lot of 'em get dumped into the rivers or the harbor."

"Well, I thank you for the information. I couldn't possibly have guessed about the horses. I couldn't possibly have mistaken the dung. Now, I need to find lodging. My train leaves in the morning."

The guard turned away silently, and Pieter headed off toward what he thought to be Grand Central.

§

Pieter Bauer did not endanger his health by staying in the festering city. Coming from a small village in southwest Germany, he was hardly prepared for the shock of a city the size of New York, to say nothing of its unhealthy environment. He thought the city might well fall prey to any of several nasty diseases: cholera, typhus, smallpox, various influenzas, diphtheria, yellow fever, tuberculosis, and on and on.

He found the New York Central ticket office, after stopping a few more people to get directions, bought a one-way seat to Chicago, and noted what information there was on lodging for the night. There would be no going back. He had learned it from newspaper ads at home and heard it reinforced on the ship: opportunity awaited the brave and the industrious in the American West. He wondered what lay behind the 'brave' thing. He wondered if he were brave and industrious enough. The promises were so extravagant as to remind older readers of promotion of the 'gold fever' thirty years earlier. Pieter, of course, had no knowledge of that deceptive campaign and its largely unrequited result. So, it would be the West. But where?

Not until the voyage to New York, along with hundreds of other Germans plus Norwegians, Swedes, and Danes, had Pieter heard of a place in Dakota Territory called Griggs, a place, which, as described by excited passengers who had never seen the village, sounded enough like Bierstadt to maintain Pieter's interest. Wound up in the excitement of starting a new life in this young country, Pieter didn't sufficiently consider the other passengers' lack of firsthand knowledge of Griggs.

Pieter Bauer was the first member of his family to seek a fresh start in the New World after the death of his father. The family had developed a plan, but it was a plan that depended on Pieter's success. It was, without doubt, an awesome responsibility to place on a young man, alone in a new world, with little formal education or practical experience.

But Anna Maria had no alternative. Pieter may have been an adequate apprentice to shoemaking at his father's side, but at this stage in his career, he could never make the kind of money that Georg Bauer had, income sufficient to support a family of six. So, his mother sent him off with the promise that the rest of the family would join him once he set up himself as a shoemaker somewhere in America.

Before Pieter left, Anna Maria came to him with a dire warning that must have struck him as nearly overwhelming. The little savings left in her purse, plus what she might make as a servant to a rich family in Bierstadt, would not support the family for more than a few months. If, she cautioned him sternly, if she could keep up a degree of frugality that the health of three young children could bear, Pieter had only a year to a year and a half to make a go of it in America. So, she insisted, he needed to be quick about his business, first as scout then as financial anchor. If he didn't succeed? Anna Maria dared not consider of that possibility.

3 DAUGHTERS

Carolyn Sofia Profit. A daughter of different fathers. In the first instance, the last of four daughters born to Samuel Allen Profit and Abigail Constance Lee of Syracuse, New York. About that second 'father' in a moment.

A tinkerer and frustrated inventor, Sam's most recent small-scale efforts proved insufficient to support a large family. He couldn't find a market for his obsessions, about which Abigail could be patient one day and another not. But Sam knew someone in Griggs, an old friend and a man familiar with Sam's industriousness and ambition who counseled change and opportunity. The vast wheat-growing plains that covered the Dakotas, Nebraska, Kansas, and reached north into Saskatchewan should appeal to a pump manufacturer like Sam Profit, the acquaintance argued with impeccable logic.

'Think of it, Sam,' his friend Arthur had counseled. 'There's your market. All that wheat will need water. That, and a man on the verge of a breakthrough with a revolutionary industrial pump; one who knows how to make water move from one place to another ... My friend, you would be a perfect fit to bring prosperity to Griggs. You've got a growing family. Just *think* of all that room out West for your young family to grow and prosper.'

Both flattered and curious, Sam Profit considered the idea for about two seconds, he later recounted the decision to friends, before presenting the idea to Abigail. That was a mistake. He should not have been surprised to find her noticeably less enthusiastic than him or Arthur.

"I have a home here in Syracuse, one that I happen to know quite well and like very much. We have growing daughters who have friends—classmates. Everyone cautions against making such a drastic change in young girls' and boys' lives. They resent it and don't adjust well to an unfamiliar environment. Syracuse is a big city. What's Griggs? Not even a town, you say. And one more thing. What about the Indian wars? They haven't ended, have they?"

That was sufficient to decide Sam Profit to sit on the idea for a time, bring it up now and then, he thought, get her used to it gradually. He didn't have an answer about the Indian wars, but that subject was central to another family decision in the making. Although, in that situation there could be no debate.

§

Abigail Constance Lee. The Interior Department of the United States dispatched George Lee, Abigail's father, a lawyer, and employee of the Bureau of Indian Affairs, to western New York where, eventually, Abigail was born. Lee was to oversee relations with the Six Nations—the Mohawk, Cayuga, Onondaga, Oneida, Seneca and Tuscarora.

His instructions were puzzling. The department directed him not to defend local tribes against white intrusion, as one might have expected of an agency charged by Congress to *protect* Indian rights. More to the point, the department expected Lee, by any means necessary, including subterfuge, to assure that Indian treaty rights did not adversely affect white property holders.

Lee knew the history of the region and past agreements between the tribes and the U.S. government. He had come to believe that all of it was just that—history. His charge, as given him and with which he had no disagreement, was to move forward, not backward. That ended any doubts he may have harbored.

The Lees settled in western New York where in years to come George and Elizabeth's daughter, Abigail, would meet and marry the afore mentioned Samuel Profit. Abigail and Samuel, in turn, produced those four daughters, the last of whom was Carolyn Sofia.

§

Regard the 'daughter' of a different father. At age 18, which she would become in 1887, and subject to the society's review, Carolyn Profit would qualify for membership in The Daughters of the American Revolution (DAR), a lineage-based organization for women directly descended from a person involved in achieving American independence. Carolyn's would-be sponsoring ancestor (that different father)? A private in the Virginia militia named Ezra Allen, a young man unremarkable in history and family lore except for the awful winter he and hundreds of other patriots spent at Valley Forge, Pennsylvania, with General George Washington.

The 'Lee' in her mother's line could offer additional proof of Carolyn's right to membership had it placed her within the Custis-Lee family of Virginia, which included George Washington's wife, Martha Custis, as well as Robert E. Lee. But to trace the zig-zag lines of Allens and Custis-Lees until they reached Carolyn Profit would require an extended genealogical essay, an enterprise that awaits another storyteller at another time, as does, similarly, the lives and loves of Carolyn's siblings and Konrad Bauer's sisters.

4 CASTLE GARDEN

Anna Maria Bauer was not an educated woman in the formal sense, but she was a clever woman. She knew her children would need to assimilate quickly in America if they were to get ahead. While the younger ones slept, she and Pieter had discussed this point late into the evenings before he left.

At market in Bierstadt, she had heard what the brochures enticing Germans and others to emigrate had to say. She couldn't read them herself, but she had an intuitive feel for their truths, which were few, and their exaggerations, which were many. Of one thing she was certain: the most difficult test for all of them would begin with the customs and health inspections when they reached America.

§

"Where does Pieter live, *Mutti*?" Konrad asked his mother.

"Don't worry, *Liebchen*. I'm sure we'll find his home."

She saw no reason to offer confusing directions now ... still so far from North Dakota.

"And you must say 'Peter' from now on, Konrad. We're in America. Speak English!"

"But I don't know any *Englisch*."

"It's 'Peter.' *Verstehst du?*"

"Yes, *Mutti*."

"Say it, Konrad. 'Peter.'"

"Pater."

"No! 'Peter'!"

"Puh ... Puh ... Peh ..."

"Oh, never mind, never mind. We'll practice later," Anna Maria said in exasperation.

§

From the moment the Bauers stumbled and swayed down the gangplank and into the 'Kastel' for immigration processing, their legs wobbly and unsure after days at sea, each rejoiced in one thing: they were off the ship!

Yes, they were ashore in America, but somehow the place didn't matter. Irrelevant. Dry land was everything. It could have been Turkey, Italy, or Norway. But the ground still undulated. When they stood still, their bodies seemed to sway. In time that would change. Another, more immediate change? Konrad had stopped vomiting.

Anna Maria Bauer saw the white-frocked orderlies—nurses, actually—and the cloth screens the orderlies and doctors, presumably the men were doctors, moved first in front of, then behind. She knew that meant health examinations, and she worried they would refuse entry to Konrad, so frail and white; they'd all have to go back. But to what, she wondered. The thought so frightened her it nearly caused *her* to vomit.

"Next," she heard someone say impatiently. It seemed so much like a German word, *nächste*.

'All right,' she confirmed the meaning as the line moved forward, 'that's another word in English that I've learned.' There would soon be others.

On the other side of a high, varnished, wooden gate that hung via swinging hinges a man in a black uniform sat on a high stool before a desk that slanted toward his lap. In one hand he held a pen, and with the other, palm down, he held open a large book on his desk that she assumed listed the passengers.

"Next!" he shouted, this time beyond impatience.

There it was again; he was speaking to her. She pushed her youngsters ahead as though she were herding a flock of geese.

"Name?" the man said, staring worriedly at the Bauer teens who had surrounded his stool.

"Get back!" he shouted at them. They didn't know the words, but they'd seen the look before.

"Name?" he repeated once the youngsters had returned to their mother's side.

'Yes, *der Name!*' she thought to herself quietly while smiling outwardly. She had grasped it intuitively, just as with 'next.'

"Bauer. Anna Maria, Marta, Louise, and Konrad Bauer," she said with growing confidence, pronouncing them carefully lest any mistake or misunderstanding doom their chance for admission.

The man paused, searching the book with his finger.

"Residence?"

"*Was?*" The clerk needed to clarify.

"*Deutsch?*

Anna Maria nodded.

"Aus welcher Stadt kommst Sie?"

"Bierstadt, Baden-Württemberg."

He continued his search.

"Let me see your papers, your passports," he said, finally, holding out his free hand.

"*Papiere!*"

Anna Maria dug into her handbag and produced the family's papers.

More scrutiny. Then, with no fanfare, he handed Anna Maria a small card and instructed them, silently pointing his finger, to follow a yellow line on the floor that led toward the dreaded, white-cloth screens. He didn't say, 'Welcome to America!'

She only heard, "Next!" as he shouted at the people who stood behind them in line.

One of the nurses beckoned the family to a row of chairs in front of one of the screens.

"Name? *Name?*"

Anna Maria flushed from fear.

"Bauer," she said quietly, as though that might prevent the inevitable. Pieter had warned his mother that the health examination would decide whether they could remain in America.

"Mother," he had pled, "they won't take you if you don't pass. Make sure no one coughs or sneezes."

He hadn't thought to add that no one should throw up! That she remembered, and it froze her in fear to think that Konrad might do just that. Then she smiled, thinking he might do it all over one of those orderly's or doctor's shoes.

"Anna Maria Bauer?"

"Yes."

"Are these your children?" The nurse employed gestures to convey her question.

That took Anna Maria by surprise, and she thought of answering sarcastically, 'Of course,' but she backed down and merely said, very quietly, "Yes."

"The doctor will see each of you alone. Do you understand?"

"Yes."

"Please go in," she instructed Anna Maria and pointed to the end of the screen. There were chairs for the children while they waited their turns.

The medical section was part of a large, fenced pen with guards stationed at each gate, one opening on each side of the rough square. The fencing reminded Anna Maria of pictures and paintings she'd seen of the American West. Cowboys herding and branding cattle.

'We're the cattle,' she realized.

Behind the screen a man in a white frock with a stethoscope hanging from behind his neck greeted her. He held a clipboard and pen.

"Name?"

"Bauer."

"Anna Maria?"

"Yes."

"Sit, please, and loosen your blouse—your shirt." He made a motion of unbuttoning his shirt. "I must listen to your heart and lungs."

She did as he instructed.

The business end of the stethoscope felt cold against her warm skin. She had begun to perspire from anxiety.

"Breathe deeply," he instructed by taking deep breaths himself.

She did so and followed the same instruction as he moved the stethoscope from place to place on her chest, then instructed her to lean forward while he listened to her heart and lungs from her back.

"Fine," he said. "You may fix your blouse and then see the orderly outside.

The doctor repeated the procedure with the girls with the same satisfactory result. Konrad saw him last, as he was the youngest.

The doctor immediately noted the pallor of his skin.

"When did you eat last? ... What is your name?"

Konrad sat transfixed, bathed in fear and on the verge of vomiting again.

The doctor scanned his clipboard.

"*Name?*" he asked, finally.

"Konrad," the boy replied, barely above a whisper.

The doctor walked to the end of the screen. He motioned to Anna Maria that she should return behind the flimsy barrier.

"Do you speak English? ... *Sprechen Sie Englisch?*"

"*Ein bisschen.*"

She wondered if he wanted to speak only in German.

"Has the boy been ill?" he asked. "He's very pale. I'm concerned he might be anemic ... *anämisch*. In that case, I can't admit him."

Anna Maria understood only the words 'can't' and 'admit.' She panicked.

"*Seekrank*! Seasick!" she pleaded. "He *seekrank* ... total."

Anna Maria began to cry. What could she say to convince this man in the white frock, who had the power to end their American dream, that they couldn't possibly go back to Germany?

"*Tot! Mein Mann ist tot!*" and she sliced across her throat with her hand.

Then, having no more words, she pointed to Konrad, who had been frightened by her neck slice, and undulated her hand and arm in a horizontal waving motion, over and over.

'*Seekrank*'! The word had suddenly come to him. The doctor thought for a moment, then called over one of the nurse/orderlies and spoke to her quietly. She went to a cabinet behind Konrad, returned and handed a small box to the doctor. He looked at Anna Maria.

"This for ..." and he undulated his hand just as Anna Maria had a moment earlier. "This for ..." and he pretended to retch. "One each day or when he is sick." He made the waving motion again.

She nodded and took the box.

Finally, he listened to Konrad's heart and lungs.

"Welcome to America!" he said as he rose from his stool. After signaling to Konrad that he could button his shirt, he handed Anna Maria a card on which he had written something. Then, in a dismissive wave of his hand, he motioned the pair around the screen to where the girls waited.

One of the orderlies pointed to a man who stood next to one of the gates and pointed the family in that direction.

His mother took Konrad's hand and the four walked smartly to the man at the gate. He looked at the card, then Anna Maria, then Konrad, then back to the card. He repeated his head movements several times. With each perusal of the card and then back the family, his head bobbed up and down in a clownish way.

Konrad giggled. It was his first normal behavior since stepping aboard the *Belgenland* in Antwerp.

PART II
FLOWERING

5   'DAKOTA'

Despite the exigencies of a civil war, an optimistic Congress looked to the future. And what a future! Providential forces were at play, Jonas Griggs was fond of saying.

Following the lead set by the Lincoln-Whig-Free Soil-Unionist agenda, the Republican majority passed two complementary measures—the homestead and transcontinental railroad acts—that played larger than life roles in filling out the United States and completing Thomas Jefferson's dream.

The Homestead Act of 1862 gave more than 160 million acres of free public land, most of it west of the Mississippi River, to 1.6 million homesteaders. Some of those homesteaders would need towns, places to gather, places to buy needed staples and specialty items when available and affordable, and they got one! The settlement of Griggs in the Dakota Territory, which began small but quickly grew exponentially, owed its name to one of those homesteaders, the afore mentioned Jonas Griggs of Vermont, a man with a growing family in a small place and, most importantly, an itch.

The Pacific Railway Act, passed the same year as the Homestead bill, led to the construction of a series of transcontinental railroads over the last third of the 19th century. Those lines created a nationwide transportation network that united the country by rail and brought those homesteaders to places like the Dakota Territory and elsewhere in the West.

Quite likely 'Dakota' and Griggs would not have come to the attention of Pieter Bauer absent the government's charter of the Northern Pacific (NP) Railway Company in July 1864, which opened unimagined acres of land for farming, ranching, lumbering, and mining. Newspapers chronicled the boom.

§

The Bismarck *Tribune*, March 25, 1890—
The larger entity from which the two Dakotas were carved (named for a branch of the Sioux tribes) had been the northernmost part of the Louisiana Purchase, as well as the southernmost part of Rupert's Land acquired when the boundary shifted to the 49th parallel. 'Dakota' continued as part of the Minnesota and Nebraska

territories until it came into its own in March 1861. 'Dakota' became two new states in November 1889.

Settlement of the northern plains began in earnest when the westbound NP built out to the Missouri River in 1872 and 1873. Rail lines had already pushed westward from Minnesota into 'Dakota' by 1871.

The NP, like other lines employing a similar combination of public and private funding, successors to the internal-improvements-Whiggery platform of Henry Clay and Abraham Lincoln, succeeded wildly. In checkerboard fashion, the federal government kept every other section of land on either side of the line, call them red, then gave them away to homesteaders. The company used its federal land grants, the opposite squares to the government's sections in that metaphorical checkerboard, call them black, as security to borrow money to build the rail system. At first, to speed construction, the company sold much of its holdings at low prices to land speculators to realize quick cash profits and to end sizable annual tax bills.

Along and near its line, new towns such as Griggs sprang up to serve the settlers, the tracklaying crews, and other, sometimes rowdy frontier citizens. The NP reached Fargo early in June 1872. That town and Bismarck both began as rough-and-tumble railroad communities.

These were settlement boom times. In northern 'Dakota' it took place between 1879 and 1886 when over 100,000 people entered the territory. The majority were homesteaders, others large, highly mechanized, well capitalized (company) farms. These operations made a lot of people very rich and helped publicize the northern frontier.

> The Bismarck *Tribune*, March 26, 1890—
> Ethnic variety characterizes the new settlements. Most of the newcomers are German and Scandinavian immigrants who bought the land cheaply and raised large families. Norwegians are the largest single group and, after 1885, desperate and ambitious Germans came from enclaves in the Russian Ukraine.
> Why Scandinavians and Germans? The Northern Pacific had opened colonization offices in Germany and Scandinavia to attract farmers with cheap package transportation and purchase deals. Years later, when land values soared and railroad executives sought security in long-term investments, they judged the sale of land at wholesale prices a mistake, but it was too late.
> The climate of Dakota Territory, while very cold in winter, is suitable for the wheat in high demand in eastern cities and Europe. The success of the NP from 1871 to 1890 was thus based on the abundant crops and the attraction of settlers to the Red River Valley along the Minnesota-'Dakota' border. It is a symbiotic relationship. Farmers ship huge quantities of wheat to Minneapolis and buy the equipment, including the irrigation pumps that make wheat production possible.
> The wheat boom aids small towns in the territory to prosper, and it performs the same function for the state. As the population grew, so did the demand for skilled craftsmen; shoemaking ranks near the top.

Pieter did not know Sam Profit or the Profit Pump Manufactory, but both men came to know the value of wheat faming in creating wealth and providing security for families in the 'Dakota.'

§

Griggs, North Dakota. The 'boondocks,' some might say of it. 'Classic' small town America, positivists would counter. Mostly, though, an inquisitor would learn: 'Never heard tell of it.'

True enough. Griggs wasn't much in 1882. So, what made the town the destination for a desperate family from southwest Germany and another from Syracuse, New York? One might also ask the same of the other townspeople. But their reasons for coming to Griggs, doubtless fascinating, are not the subject of this story.

Whatever one thought of its size or contribution to the nation or the world, Griggs was the unlikeliest place for romance to blossom between a DAR with its imprimatur of elitism and a German boy from Bierstadt with a missing pedigree. Whatever his ancestry might have been, by the time the *Belgenland* plowed westward across the Atlantic, various warring armies had trampled Konrad Bauer's imaginary coat of arms, and very real potatoes, turnips, and rutabagas into the mud of the Eurasian steppes somewhere between the Black and Baltic seas. Nothing remained for which to return.

§

If one were to look at an overhead photo of Griggs between 1882 and 1890, they would note the following. Nearly every building and appurtenance in town was of wood: houses, sidewalks (where they existed), churches, water towers and schools. They would also note one or two commercial buildings of solid brick and concrete. Inside those 'magnificent' edifices, shoppers would find dry goods, ladies ready-to-wear, men's and boy's clothing, groceries, and flour. The dry goods, hardware, men's and women's furnishings, and grocery departments occupied the first floor; rugs and carpeting the second; and in the basement, general storage.

The lone grain elevator and associated storage buildings stood next to the railroad line. That building and Sam Profit's pump manufactory also appeared to be brick and concrete. The other notable feature as seen from above were dirt streets and the occasional solitary tree. Wind and snow breaks provided by lines of trees strategically planted awaited future generations.

§

Of course, Griggs was more than structures. If one were to visit the town in the 1880s, or even later, it would not escape them that the settlement could legitimately brag of an artistic sensibility. Yes, there were residents who appreciated art in the traditional sense, framed family portraits or landscapes on someone's living room or bedroom wall.

But if art in the traditionalist sense wasn't a resident or visitor's interest, those folks could give way to an artistic appreciation of the surrounding environment. The residents of Griggs had the good fortune to live amid a natural outdoor sports arena with every conceivable challenge to take up, whether in summer—hiking, horseback riding, fishing, swimming, camping—or throughout the very long winters—cross-country skiing, sledding, and skating.

Those activities, no matter how pleasing and fulfilling, were not what brought the Samuel Profit family to Griggs. No, what did supply the incentive was an unaesthetic object—its design artistic in a perverse sense—essential to move water vertically and then horizontally in a virtually flat landscape: the pump or, to be precise, simple and complex pumps of every type and corresponding purpose.

Sam Profit was a pump man who believed he could build what Dakotans needed to move water from deep aquifers, and then distribute it across miles and miles of wheat fields, while at the same time turning Griggs into a notable manufacturing town and making his family a fortune. First, however, Sam had to learn, practice, and master the challenges of economics and politics.

§

Young Carolyn arrived with her family in the territory just in time for that eager student to grasp the principle of action and reaction, not only from her schoolbooks, but from life. Carolyn took to history like none of her siblings. In the 8th grade, which required students to learn the history of 'Dakota,' she came to understand important fundamentals about her emerging and energetic new state.

Action and reaction. Carolyn learned that the population surge, which the railroad had stimulated, increased the demand for meat, which spurred cattle ranching. In turn, the surge in population and ranching intensified the demand for agriculture, and wheat became the territory's main cash crop.

Then, calamity. Economic hardship. The Profit family couldn't have arrived at a less opportune moment. Declining demand elsewhere in the 1880s lowered wheat prices. On top of that, the territory reeled from drought. When she was sure he wouldn't notice, Carolyn learned over her father's shoulder to watch how he struggled to manufacture his pumps under the weight of problems he couldn't control.

Ironically, the drought presented an opportunity for irrigation, but Sam Profit's production was insufficient to match the demand and support his large family. From their bedrooms, the girls listened night after night as their parents discussed the family's increasingly dire circumstance in hushed, tense voices.

But droughts don't last forever, nor do tough times. Political insurgency, followed by consolidation in the 1890s, characterized the response to the economic problems. The Republican Party, which now included the enthusiastic support of Sam Profit, managed to wrest back control of the state from inexperienced Independents and Democrats in 1894.

> The Bismarck *Tribune*, November 16, 1894—
> Controlled by conservatives, North Dakota's Republican government encouraged investment by establishing liberal banking, regulatory, and taxation policies; to support their policies, conservatives argued that capitalists would not

> invest in North Dakota unless state government did its part to diminish risk and enhance profits.
>
> Though severely criticized by progressive Democrats and Independents, both relegated to the political sidelines in 1894, the Republican approach resulted in new industrial development. Large lignite mines opened, and local brickworks and flour mills soon dotted the state. And the *Profit Pump Manufactory,* which received help from the new economic strategy, began to 'pump out' a volume of product sufficient to meet the state's expanding economy. The railroad industry was not sitting still, either. Bolstered by completion of the Great Northern in 1887 and the Soo Line in 1893, branch lines fostered new towns.

Smart people knew that Republican nostrums minus thoughtful, realistic policies wouldn't last forever. By the time the latest reaction set in, Sam Profit had not only *found* his footing, but he had also become fleet of foot.

In the loft, the girls slept more soundly.

6 FOOTWEAR & PUMPS

Some of Germany's—and the world's—finest shoemakers practiced their craft in the state of Baden-Württemberg. Was Georg Bauer among that elite? There's no way to answer that question; perhaps it wasn't even a useful question to ask. Pieter certainly thought highly of his father's skill or he would not have considered apprenticing with him. But his father's sudden passing and other factors added to a series of setbacks to Pieter's expected career in Bierstadt.

§

Pieter Bauer and other boys who aspired to become master craftsman could enter into an apprenticeship only after confirmation (age 12–16), which, in Pieter's case, occurred at the family's Lutheran (Evangelical) parish.

Apprenticeship lasted several years. At its conclusion, the master presented the young man with a *Gesellenbrief,* an apprentice diploma or, in the case of the journeyman, which was the next step in the process, a certificate of competence.

A journeyman spent from 2–4 years, depending on the trade, traveling the country and working for various masters in the craft. On his return home, the journeyman produced a 'Master Piece,' its quality (acceptance) subject to the judgment of all the master artisans of his trade in the area. Only then was the candidate able to become a master himself.

The word artisan or craftsman sounded impressive, and it stood for a status in Pieter's village worthy of achievement. Craftsmen were middle class, although most of them farmed, or at least tended a garden to help feed their families. Middle class, yes, but craftsmen faced limited upward mobility.

In Pieter's case, however, there were barriers to his gaining that status. According to guild 'law' he would have to consider apprenticing with someone other than his father. Moreover, if Bierstadt already had two shoemakers—Georg Bauer being one—and the town council felt a third was unnecessary, no other shoemaker could become a citizen in that town or even live there as a *Hintersasse,* a resident without citizenship. Not even Pieter!

Those issues, and others, became moot when Georg's sudden death decided everything. In life, neither Georg nor Pieter had the broader awareness, the ability to look beyond their limited business environment to see that mass production (factory) techniques in the late nineteenth century were eroding the craft process. Thus, by the time of Georg's passing, handicraft shoemaking was on its way to volume shoemaking and craftsmen on their way from shoemakers to shoe repairmen.

§

Pieter Bauer never completed his apprenticeship, the journeymen's travel, or the required 'Master Piece.' Georg's death meant the family needed a replacement income or succumb to destitution, starvation, and death. Anna Maria and Pieter decided the only possibility for the family's survival lay with emigration. Together, they made the difficult decision to send him to America ahead of the rest of the family.

That decision was less problematic from Pieter's point of view than one might assume. He had learned the shoemaking craft well enough at his father's side, and in truth he had no use for those journeyman years on the road working for strangers. Nor was he inclined to join a guild required of those with 'master' status. On the other hand, America, free of such restrictions, had great appeal beyond its necessity.

By the time Pieter (now Peter) arrived in Griggs, the change to mass production had already eaten away at his opportunity to practice the craft he had spent years learning. The shop he eventually opened was a repair shop. Shoemaking now belonged to distant, industrialized cities.

Nonetheless, the people in Griggs were grateful to have a repairman with Peter's skill. It was financially difficult for people in this farming community to buy new shoes. The young man from Bierstadt seemed a perfect fit. Also, Pieter knew leather, so, additional opportunities existed for harnesses, saddles, saddlebags, and women's handbags.

Elsewhere, another skilled newcomer was struggling to show himself as a useful addition to the community.

§

Sam Profit did not grow into his profession through a structured tradition anything like that of late 19th century Germany. Nevertheless, as an inventor and manufacturer he had 'mastered' a great deal of technical and practical information about pumps. Now, he needed to learn to apply his mechanical devices to the needs of 'Dakota' wheat farmers.

One week after he moved his family to Griggs, Sam met with local farmers at their Grange to learn how his existing pumps might—or might not—meet their needs. Should his inventions be insufficient, he asked, what adaptations or innovative technology would?

They told him they were in trouble. They needed more highly powered pumps than those already in use to get the water out of deep aquifers, and then some horizontal designs to power water to huge sprinklers, plowed furrows, and to sustain efficient drip systems.

Two weeks later Sam met again with the farmers. He explained the choices he had made for them and took a few questions. He also brought along some models, which he believed would illustrate the points he wanted to make. He started with centrifugal pumps.

"The pumps you already use are probably centrifugal ones without the latest technology. Centrifugal pumps, both vertical and horizontal are the most common type for the sort of irrigation you apparently need. Without admitting to immodesty, I believe you will find my pumps superior to any you have."

A man wearing bib overalls in the third row stood with his hand up.

"Yes, you have a question?"

"Sure do, Mr. Profit. What's the new gadgetry you talkin' about?"

"What's your name, sir? I want to get to know my neighbors."

"It's like yours, Sam ... Sam Butler."

"Well, Sam Butler, the answer is electricity!"

The room exploded with whispered astonishment.

"You need power for those expansive fields of yours. Applying electricity to your pumps will change everything for you. Let me explain, briefly ...

"We use centrifugal pumps to get water from reservoirs, lakes, streams and shallow wells. We also use them to boost negative flow in irrigation pipelines. Put another way, to raise a liquid, you need the vertical centrifugal pump; the horizontal version induces flow once you overcome gravity ...

"A simple mechanism applies to both. A centrifugal pump converts rotational energy ... and this is where electricity comes in ... to energy that moves a fluid. While passing through the impeller, a set of spinning blades, the fluid gains both velocity and pressure ...

In 1820, two men, Faraday and Henry, invented a primitive electric motor. A wire spinning near a magnet could produce an electric current—the principle of the generator ...

"Then, the most significant improvement came in 1870 when a Belgian inventor devised a dynamo that produced a steady, direct current well-suited to powering motors—a discovery that generated a burst of enthusiasm about electricity's potential. I have incorporated this technology into my pumps."

Another of the men raised his hand.

"Yes, sir. Question? And tell me your name."

"Charles Atkins. Our aquifers are so deep here, so, I'm not sure your centrifugal pump can get the water up, even with an electric motor ... dynamo ... whatever. You have an alternative?"

"For deep wells, you might want to consider a 'deep-well turbine' pump ...

"Turbine pump efficiencies are comparable to or greater than most centrifugal pumps, but they come with a couple of disadvantages: more expensive than centrifugal pumps and more difficult to inspect and repair ...

"If you are trying to pump water up more than 10.3 meters, then you need to put the pump at the bottom of the water supply. The pump can push the water with a pressure that is greater than atmospheric pressure ...

"My well is about 100 feet. This is roughly 30 meters. The pump is at the bottom of the well. There are 100 feet of pipe from the pump up to the surface. There are also 100 feet of electrical wiring from the surface going down to the pump ...

"It is relatively straightforward for a pump to create enough pressure to raise water by 30 meters or more. It is also relatively straightforward to create piping that can handle this much pressure and hold the water ...

"We get good water at that depth. Others, too, with wells from 60 to 100 feet. That water is of excellent quality and flow for drinking and household purposes, but you will certainly need more powerful pumps for your fields ...

"How deep are your aquifers, on average?"

"Bernie Taylor here, Mr. Profit. I do most of the diggin' in and around Griggs, so, I 'spose I'm the one ought to know."

"So, do ya, Bernie?" someone shouted from the back of the room. "Can ya answer the man or not?"

The room broke into laughter.

"Hold it, fellas. I'm sure Mr. Taylor can answer my question."

"Yur durn right I can! The answer is they're about the same as your well, Mr. Profit, but some could be as much as 300–400 feet."

The room broke into cheers and laughter.

"Okay, that's turbine territory, probably staged. I'll explain that in a minute. If you decide on one of those, and I hope you'll pick from those I make right here in Griggs, let me make two points about what to expect, just to get your feet movin' ...

"First, the use of vertical turbine pumps for well water is common. The depth of turbine pumps ranges from around 100 feet all the way up to around 1,000 feet; settings between 200 and 400 feet are common. They're used all over the country. Sometimes I can't keep up with the orders. Those of you with boys who've started working for me know that ...

"Second, staging. We can also build these pumps in a series; that is, more than one impeller. Each new impeller increases the amount the pump can produce while the flow is unchanged. For example, if I design a single-stage turbine (one impeller) to produce 1,000 gallons per minute at 100 feet, then adding a second identical stage would double that."

The Grange meeting broke up without the promise of immediate sales. Had Sam thought he would be signing contracts that night, he didn't know his audience. It would take one or two of the farmers to buy a pump or two, and then spread the word, yea or nay to Sam Profit's profits.

"Any luck?" Abigail asked when Sam closed the door.

"Some nibbles. No serious bites. But I think they liked the bait," he replied with a wink and a smile.

7   'HOTTEST STUFF'

Bob: *How do you do, madam, I'm a coal man.*
    Frankie: *No, thank you, I have a coal man.*
    Bob: *Yeah, but you don't understand; I am the coal man.*
    Frankie: *Makes no difference.*
    Bob: *I'm just a coal man, sellin' the hottest stuff in town.*

I'm just a coal man, baby; in the winter I'm good to have around.
Now, I sell coal, and I sell ice,
In the wintertime a coal man's mighty nice,
Now, I'm just a coal man, sellin' the hottest stuff in town.

    Frankie: *You say you're just a coal man...*

Bob: That's right, baby.
Frankie: ... selling the hottest stuff in town.
Bob: Um-hum.
Frankie: Well, my present coal man serves me,
Whether I'm up or whether I'm down.
Bob: I can do that.
Frankie: He makes his delivery...
Bob: Uh-huh.
Frankie: ... right on time.
Bob: Sure.
Frankie: And his product contains no slack or lime.
Bob: Neither does mine.
Frankie: So how come you say you're such a coal man...
Bob: Um-hmm.
Frankie: ... sellin' the hottest stuff in town?
Bob: Um-hmm.
Frankie: Now, listen, I'm satisfied with my form of heat.
Bob: Yeah.
Frankie: In the winter I drop and toast my feet.
Bob: Um-hmm.
Frankie: I've had him quite a while and I'll keep him still.
Bob: Um-hmm.
Frankie: Sometimes I say I'll change, but I don't think I will.
Bob: Now, I'm a coal salesman, and here's a tip.
I've got a sales talk that's bustin' my lip.
My merchandise is extra clean.
So, take a look, baby, it's the best you've ever seen.
It handles well, no clinkers form,

A Most Improbable Union 59

Make you feel good in the worst kind of storm;
Takin' care of your comfort is my mission.
Heh! Baby, is your heatin' apparatus in good condition?
Frankie: *You say you're just a coal man...*
Bob: *That's right, baby.*
Frankie: *... selling the hottest stuff in town.*
Bob: *Uh-huh!*
Frankie: *You also said in the wintertime...*
Bob: *What?*
Frankie: *... you're a lovely thing to have around.*
Bob: *Like to be.*
Frankie: *Your sales talk...*
Bob: *Um-hmm.*
Frankie: *... was mighty fine.*
Bob: *Yes.*
Frankie: *Tell me more, brother, I might change my mind!*
Bob: *I'm here!*
Frankie: *Since you're such a big shot coal man,*
Selling the hottest stuff in town!
Bob: *Now, mama, papa's just a little ol' coal man,*
Sellin' the hottest stuff in town.
Now, baby, I'm just a coal man,
In the winter, I'm good to have around.
I'll take your order and fill your bin,
Go get it cleaned out and I'll put it right in,
'Cause I'm just a coal man,
Sellin' the hottest stuff in town!
I'm just a coal man,
Sellin' the hottest stuff in town!
I say, sellin' the hottest stuff in town!

Frankie*: Sold, brother, sold!'*

8 BORN GO-GETTER

By the end of the century, the seasick steerage passenger from the *Belgenland* had grown into a handsome young man of medium height and build. He turned twenty-eight in 1898. His ready smile and optimistic demeanor had drawn him easily into associations and friendships with townspeople of all ages, types, and place. It was the stuff of a born go-getter.

No one in Griggs in 1898 could have imagined the pitiful *Belgenland* wretch whose only thoughts were of himself and the torture his mother inflicted for reasons his spinning head couldn't fathom. That should not be surprising. Seasickness can lay low the best of men and women, let alone an eleven-year-old boy. Once Konrad left Castle Garden and began to experience and appreciate

New York—the smell not so much—he rallied quickly. Indeed, he came to enjoy the city so much he was loathe to leave! That was the Konrad who had always been there, the Konrad who grew easily into a positive achiever.

Konrad (now Conrad) had found a niche for himself in Griggs. He had worked part time during the last two years of high school. Since then, a series of jobs came along, but none supplied the kind of permanence a solid future required. And, of course, the future included the thought of a family.

One of his part time jobs had been with Peter. The older brother had built a workshop/store adjoining the Bauer home—literally attached to it—on the corner of Second and Prairie, one block off Main. By the time Conrad was free of school, Peter's business had also taken on craft leathers—harnesses and so forth.

He admired his older brother's skill, which had kept the family alive during his growing years, but he had no desire to work permanently alongside Peter. Conrad realized that neither leather nor working for someone were advancing the independent life he desired. His future belonged elsewhere.

That future nearly came to fruition when he landed a job at Sam Profit's manufactory after finishing his schooling. He learned various forms of metal fabrication, but, again, as in leather, making pumps for someone else with no prospect of advancement to position, was not Conrad's idea of a place for future independence and security.

§

Before graduating high school, Conrad had taken stock of the importance of the fuel that made possible the industrialization of the country, raising it to a world power and laying fortunes at the feet of investors. Other aspects of the energy requirements of Griggs prompted Conrad's interest in coal at the same time his satisfaction with leather and metal fabrication waned.

Griggs had one coal dealer, an elderly man with a small crew. Conrad thought that replacing Merton Belcher, should he retire, might be the key to his dream of self-sufficiency. It was the only business in Griggs that offered the prospect of instant security. He reckoned that most people in Griggs had little interest in competing for a coal dealership.

He would present himself to Mr. Belcher as an ambitious young man able to adapt to jobs requiring different skills. He'd learn the business from the old man, and when Belcher retired, he'd in position to inherit the business.

Something else had triggered Conrad's interest in 'black gold.' When he was in high school his family had switched from wood to coal for their large kitchen stove, which was also the means of heating their home. The second-hand stove cost Peter nearly six months of hard work in his 'shop,' but it earned him the affection and gratitude of Anna Maria.

Were he to become a man of coal, a realistic man of coal, Conrad knew—some would say instinctively—he should concentrate on the micro economy of Griggs and not the mines in Wyoming, Appalachia, or the Eastern money that drove the macro coal economy. Griggs, Conrad came to believe, like thousands of homeowners back

East, should also use coal to heat their houses and cook their food.

Conrad welcomed the opportunity that lay before him. He believed the lives of the homeowners of Griggs, who suffered stoically through winters that lasted most of nine months, could, like his family, have a better life by switching from wood to coal. He'd push harder than Mr. Belcher had to expand clientele.

So, Conrad Bauer, the name he'd insisted on since graduating from high school—made it his mission to push for more coal in Griggs. Coal would help him, as the culture of that era expected, in supporting his mother, and someday, perhaps, a family of his own.

He began at Belcher after abandoning the leather and pump business. He proved a quick study, and in short order Belcher gave him the responsibility as a crew leader.

§

Consider the life of a 'coal man' as experienced by Conrad Bauer and coal men everywhere.

Deliveries were tough on a coal man's health and comfort. Deliverymen suffered from chronic back problems, even pneumonia. They breathed in coal dust all day but found that drinking milk counteracted its effects in their mouths and throats. Wet weather made a misery of deliveries. To fight off rain or snow crews wore 'wetbacks,' a kind of leather vest to keep them as dry as a mere vest could.

Deliverymen had to show adaptability and initiative, whether working inside a home or down an alley to the coal shed behind the house. Older houses were set up for basement furnaces. In that case, deliveries went into a coal bin. Crews carried long, metal conveyers (troughs) to carry the coal from the truck to the bin. They counted on gravity to do the trick, but they often had to move stubborn coal along with shovels. It all depended on the height of the truck in relation to the cellar bin.

Back at the yard, the crew loaded more product, got something to eat and drink at a café, and returned for more deliveries.

In freezing weather, deliverymen lit small fires under their truck engines to thaw them, otherwise a radiator plug might blow and cause a breakdown. The piles of coal in the yard were often frozen solid, making it hard to get shovels into it. Crews built fires to warm themselves and thaw the coal.

Summer was not coal season, and there were few deliveries. Summer work mostly involved unloading coal from the rail cars and shoveling it into bays for the fall and winter.

Conrad brought new energy to the business. Mr. Belcher, a decent judge of competence, reliability, and character—if nothing else—rewarded Conrad by promoting him to run the office.

Despite all, Conrad figured coal and the possibility of ownership might well provide him a living in the future. Still, he considered coal a business, not a relationship of affection.

Affection, possibly love, although that was unclear initially, involved a young woman of his acquaintance, a schoolmate from earlier years. It could not have escaped Conrad's notice that the object of his affection was the fourth daughter of the most important businessman in

Griggs. And himself? That was the point wasn't it: Conrad Bauer, the immigrant second son of a shoemaker.

9 'ROMEO & JULIET'

Griggs High served about 70 students in 1887. Conrad Bauer had been one of them at his mother's insistence, but not Marta or Louise. Anna Maria kept Conrad's sisters at home where she could teach them to become competent homemakers. That, she believed, trumped whatever they might learn elsewhere about mathematics, geography, or science.

Anna Maria would help her children with one other necessity: citizenship. They had mastered English in grammar school; Anna Maria would home-school them on the Constitution, which she spent years mastering herself. She had sacrificed everything to bring her family safely to the America. There would be no going back to

Germany. Then surely, she thought, all of them ought to honor their new home by becoming citizens.

On the other hand, Anna Maria also expected Conrad and Peter to take care of the Bierstadt family and prepare themselves for futures with their own families. For those reasons she insisted they get as much education as possible. His mother's plan may not have suited Conrad's own ambitions, but he went along with it anyway. His character was not that of a rebel, a fortuitous trait it turned out. For he could not have expected that his willingness to obey Anna Maria would bring him into the orbit of a vivacious young woman destined to play a major role in his life.

Conrad had no difficulty deciding that among those roughly 70 students at Griggs High, Carolyn Profit, who sat in front of him in their algebra class, was the smartest and most beautiful girl among them: auburn hair, which she piled on top of her head in the style of the day; hazel eyes, sometimes green, sometimes gray—he was never quite sure; a thin, chiseled nose, which reminded him of Greek statuary; and her lips, not full but sweetly narrow.

Conrad was a bit devious in his interactions with Carolyn in that algebra class. He played dumb—not that he really needed to—a calculated gambit that persuaded Carolyn that this classmate, who had begun to take on the attributes of a handsome, if not tall, young man (shorter than Carolyn by two inches), needed help, she assumed, if he were to pass the course and perhaps move on to geometry. Regarding the latter, he decided—having passed algebra with Carolyn's help—to live his life without further 'enrichment' in mathematics.

§

Conrad Bauer's interest in Carolyn Profit, which had and would continue to exist at a distance—except for that algebra class—did not, under normal circumstance, have a promising future. The wooing of an industrialist's daughter by someone in the coal busines was not, by the nature of things in Griggs, North Dakota—or elsewhere—anything like 'Bob's' romantic, innuendo-loaded pitch to 'Frankie.'

Most any townsperson, when presented with a hypothetical, would tell a questioner that a coal delivery man, even a coal dealer, was no match for someone of Carolyn's elevation. So, was Conrad Bauer's interest in Carolyn Profit that of a social climber? Some believed it quite likely. How else to explain his reaching so high? Much of Conrad's challenge came not from any inadequacy of his, but from the reality that in the eyes of the community Carolyn's father was a producer, a man who provided jobs and put money into circulation. A worthy man in many respects.

Conrad Bauer, on the other hand, pleasant and ambitious as he might be, merely supplied a service—and a dirty one at that. The hypothetical put to townspeople might have pertained to a young man of good character, but also to one who did not supply more than a handful of jobs.

Nonetheless, if the specific were to replace the hypothetical, if love were to trump traditionally dim prospects, a glimmer of hope existed in the Profit home for the young man from Bierstadt. While contrasts in wealth and provisions of employment may have mattered to some in Griggs, would they to Carolyn Profit? Did she, too, see the world in terms of producers and non-producers?

Years later some would say it was cheeky of Conrad Bauer to think he could court out of his class. Others thought new generations of young people brought fresh ideas and vitality to a community and ought to have a chance to change things … a little—but not too much.

Before anything further happened, whether the old ways would surrender to a bold and vigorous youth, Conrad Bauer had to plot the wooing of Carolyn Profit and then show his hand. He didn't come to this project uninformed. He had read books, among them romantic stories and novels, even Shakespeare's sonnets, wherein lay all accessible secrets of pitching woo. That night in bed and at other times he approached 'Romeo and Juliet' with the drive of an entrepreneur and the curiosity of a romantic.

PART III
ARDOR

10
THE SUITOR

As parents, Abigail and Sam Profit did not conform to the idea prevalent then that a young woman must marry as soon as, or shortly after, she reached child-bearing age. Men, they instructed Phyllis, Elizabeth, Katherine, and Carolyn, were not unnecessary but necessary only when the time was right. Some who didn't know the Profits would say they were eccentric, out of touch; some who did know them might agree. But whether anyone agreed or disagreed, there was more to their behavior than eccentricity.

The protective envelope rationalized by the Profits amounted to the prolonged treatment of their daughters as though they were children, despite their being adults. Perhaps the most charitable explanations: the Profits underestimated their daughters' potentials, disrespected them, or patronized them. Physical growth progressed normally, but did the real possibility of infantilization stunt their emotional growth?

Abigail insisted on another clue to the Profits' supposed eccentricity. The young women would not attend finishing schools like St. Benedict's Academy in St. Joseph, Minnesota. The Profits believed the primary goal of most such schools was to teach young women how to get husbands, which Sam and Abigail did not believe should be the first aim of their daughters' education as they approached adulthood. But would the best laid plans of mothers and fathers be a match for those controlled by hormones?

Abigail also insisted to anyone who would listen that finishing schools emphasized social graces and de-emphasized scholarship. The proprietors of such places Abigail argued, encouraged a polished young lady to hide her intellectual prowess for fear of frightening away suitors.

"St. Benedict's purpose and aim embraced 'every useful and ornamental branch of education suitable for young ladies,'" Sam read from the school's brochure. "St. Benedict's did not seek to training girls for a career, only 'qualities to grace a home.'"

"Stop right there! Enough!" Abigail cried as Sam read aloud. 'What social graces and qualities taught at formal finishing schools were essential to life in Griggs?' she wondered.

Abigail would have none of such 'finishing.' *She* would provide the domestic requirements; the local schools would provide the education; and men would be welcome when her 'girls' were ready. Finishing school or no, Phyllis and Elizabeth, apparently undeterred by their parents' goals, would find husbands who were not in fear of intelligent partners. But Carolyn, perhaps Katherine as well, gave every appearance of having no interest in the other sex before any suitors came knocking. The other question was why suitors had not?

§

"Hello, Conrad."

Griggs's youthful businessman completed his walk to the Profit place. It was a hot day in early July, two days until the Fourth, and the thermometer, had one been available, would have read 94 degrees.

It's impossible to be certain what was on his mind that day. The heat? Probably. Romance? Probably. Was the coal man trying to elevate his standing in the community by appearing to woo the daughter of one of Griggs's wealthiest and most prominent businessmen? Possibly. Those who believed in the prominence of rational behavior would have said so.

Without dismissing love's central place in human relations, rationalists would still call love a fundamentally irrational sentiment. Other than the memory of an algebra class a decade ago and more, he had no basis to believe Carolyn felt anything for him, or for that matter he for her. If sentiment alone had motivated Conrad, rationalists would argue, he took a big risk that day; that is, unless he had a hidden *rational* purpose.

§

Conrad found Carolyn and a friend he recognized from school, Mildred Cooper, emptying the horse trough with buckets, after which logic and common sense suggested they planned to refill it and cool off in clean water. They were also in a childish mood for their ages, engaged in an activity Carolyn's parents strictly forbade when the girls *were* children. Now, however, Carolyn apparently thought herself old enough and clever enough to hide childish activity from her parents.

Soon, the girls' original purpose at the trough turned chaotic. They tired of scooping out the old water, a process that seemed especially slow. Suddenly, Carolyn splashed water onto Mildred, predictably triggering a reaction.

The pair threw down their pails and began to splash the water out with their hands. Innocent splashing became all-out warfare, including much shrieking. The 'war' had begun deliberately, of course, which was the fun of it on a hot day—if you were in a childish mood.

Conrad had strolled up the lane and onto the property just in time to see two women at play. Mildred Cooper, embarrassed by his sudden appearance and his having seen her condition, scampered down the lane toward her home. Carolyn stood firm.

She had followed Conrad's career since high school ... sort of. She remained interested in him from a distance, and it would be wrong to assume her interest was devoid of any sense of romance. Seeing him walk toward the house quickened her heart, but this was not how she had imagined a romantic breakthrough, if that was what his arrival meant. Nonetheless, wet, disheveled, her fully developed figure outlined by a dripping, clingy dress—a sight Conrad could not have overlooked—she could think of only one thing to say.

"Hello, Conrad," she repeated, bending forward, holding her arms and hands in front of those areas of her body that revealed her womanhood. Then, an odd thing happened. The closer Conrad approached—for her embarrassment seemed not to dissuade him—the more she relinquished her protection, as if by instinct.

Was it romance or advantage that Conrad looked for? His clear shyness contrasted sharply with Carolyn's forward behavior. Clearly, he had hoped to see Carolyn, but he wasn't confident enough to explain his intent in being there, or he was too shy to do so in her presence! Clearly, the sight of her had thrown him into a state of confusion So, he obfuscated. Or was his need to obfuscate a sign of something else at play?

"Is you father home? I need to speak to him," he finally blurted out.

"About what?"

More obfuscation.

"Coal. It's not too soon to refill your bin for the fall."

"Father is at work, Conrad. He won't be home until supper. You must know that. Is that why you're here, in the middle of the afternoon?"

More obfuscation.

"Yes. I suppose I lost track of the time."

"Silly man. Are you sure there wasn't another reason?"

Game over for Conrad Bauer.

"Well, I had hoped to see *you*."

"And now you have. Is there something you wanted to see me about?"

She had the shy young man trapped. When he walked up that lane thinking he might ask Sam Profit if he could court his daughter and then saw Carolyn outlined by wet clothing that left little to his imagination, he had no idea how to interact with her. Now, she had forced him to come up with an explanation. The fun she was having at his expense did not amuse him.

Suddenly, he remembered the Fourth. That was it! He moved closer to her.

"Stop right there, Conrad Bauer!"

"Oh, sorry."

"What is it, Conrad? Can't you tell me honestly why you're here?"

His courage strengthening, he came up with the answer he was sure would obscure his true purpose. He blurted it out, almost without realizing.

"Would you care to attend the Fourth of July parade with me? Perhaps we could go to the picnic together afterward?"

Carolyn blushed.

"My, you are a surprise, Mr. Conrad Bauer! You say you came to talk to Father, and now you've invited me to spend the Fourth with you. I'd be much more likely to say, 'yes,' if you told me the truth."

She had him again. He had to respond.

11 SQUEEZING CONRAD

"All right, Miss Profit. You asked for it. I came to ask for your father's permission to court you. There, I said it!"

She paused to absorb his words. A delicious smile crossed her face.

"Shouldn't you have asked *me* first? I might have said, 'no,'" she teased.

Her tacked-on sentence sailed right past the shaken young man. Bested, he continued to struggle to regain composure.

"I suppose so, but this is all so new to me. I asked my brother what I should do, and he said, 'Ask her father.'"

Carolyn, still wet from the romp in the horse trough, moved toward her suitor and held out her hand to shake his. Instead, he lifted it to his lips.

"My, oh my, aren't you a fresh one," she laughed. "Where did you learn to do that?"

"As kids, I practiced with my sisters when Mother wasn't around."

She nearly collapsed with laughter.

"All right, Mr. Bauer, we should go up to the house. You should ask Mother about the Fourth."

"What about your father?"

"I suppose you'll have to come back when he's home, if you're still interested," she teased again.

Verbal jousting with Miss Carolyn Profit would be a challenge.

§

They found Abigail Profit squeezing lemons in the kitchen.

"Mother, this is Conrad Bauer. We were in school together, and he's worked at the factory in the past."

Abigail Profit never looked his way, and instead stopped her daughter short.

"What in the world got into you out there? You know that water is not clean. What were you thinking? … Hello, Mr. Bauer," she added with a casual glance in his direction, as though he were a distraction or not present.

"I'm sorry, Mother. It was so hot!"

Abigail looked at her daughter and shrugged in resignation. Then she turned to Conrad. Finally.

"Okay, young man. What brings you here? You weren't mixed up in that water business, were you?"

Conrad's confidence had grown by the minute ... until that minute.

"Hello, Mrs. Profit," he stammered. "No Ma'am, I wasn't."

He hesitated, casting a quick glance at Carolyn.

"I came to ask Carolyn to the parade and picnic on the Fourth."

Abigail shifted her eyes back to Carolyn, who smiled sheepishly.

"Is this true, Carolyn?"

"Yes, Mother."

Carolyn felt she needed to vouch for Conrad's status in the community to justify such a request.

"Conrad works for the coal dealer in town, Mother. He knows Father. He once worked for him."

But Abigail Profit wasn't impressed.

"Really? Isn't coal a dirty job, Conrad?"

"Mother!"

"It can be, Mrs. Profit," Conrad jumped in. "But I work mostly in the office. I hope to own the business when the current owner retires."

Abigail had tried to diminish Conrad in her daughter's eyes. Carolyn saw what was happening and resented it.

"How do you know my daughter? Oh, yes, I remember now. Carolyn said you are ... were? ... a schoolmate?"

"Yes, Ma'am."

"Conrad, you should know right now I don't like that expression."

"Which expression, Ma'am."

Carolyn suddenly felt faint.

"That one!" she said sternly. "'Ma'am'! I'm not a madam!"

Abigail saw the look of embarrassment on Conrad's face and decided he needed reassuring. Her tone softened.

"Look, Conrad, it's just something I don't care to hear. It makes me sound older than I am, and I am vain," she said with a smile and touched his forearm. "Okay?"

He returned her smile.

"Sure, Mrs. Profit."

Conrad may not have noticed that Carolyn had let out a deep breath. She took his hand and squeezed it.

"Now, Carolyn, I know it's a warm day, but you need to get out of those wet clothes, or you'll catch your death. Conrad," she added curtly, addressing the obvious reason it was time for him to leave, "we'll see you on the Fourth?"

He looked at Carolyn, who smiled and nodded once her assent.

"Yes, Mrs. Profit."

Abigail Profit, briefly lost in memories of her own courting days, had forgotten to offer the lemonade.

12   EZRA ALLEN

Carolyn Profit had qualified for DAR membership when she turned eighteen. She then met all the organization's affiliate requirements. Once involved in the Daughter's activities, she decided the society might be the most important thing in her life.

Carolyn's new status as a member of the DAR had a downside, the revelation of an unfamiliar character trait that worried her mother. Carolyn had taken to boasting of her membership to friends and anyone who might listen. Abigail had issued a warning to Carolyn when she prayed her daughter was still young enough to mend her ways.

"Just you remember who you are and are not, young lady! Better climb down from that high horse of yours before you fall off! That man Allen may have been at Valley

Forge with General Washington, but he was *not* George Washington."

Having delivered the admonition, Abigail's tone and message softened.

"Honey, you're not going to have or keep many friends if you act so superior because you had an ancestor in the American Revolution. You live in a small town in North Dakota, not Boston or Philadelphia or Charlottesville. You are not that poor young soldier! *You* had nothing to do with our independence. The DAR has worthy causes. Occupy yourself with those. Besides, do we really know who ... uh ... "

"Ezra Allen, Mom."

"Well, do any of us know what 'Ezra Allen' accomplished, other than nearly starving and freezing to death in Pennsylvania? Is that a lot for you to brag about? I don't think so. Why don't you try to imagine what Private Allen went through. You know what harsh winters are like."

So, that winter became memorable for no other reason that it reminded the Profits that Carolyn's elevation had resurrected the otherwise obscure role—deservedly so, considering its passive nature—of Ezra Allen in achieving American independence. Abigail was determined to make a point of it, lest her daughter forgot her ancestor's sacrifice.

"Tell you what," Abigail said to her daughter. "I'll give you some old rags to wrap around your feet, a blanket to throw over your shoulders, and a scarf to hold down your cap, cover your ears, and tie under your chin. We'll get you ready, then I want you to go outdoors for as long as you can stand it. Our gauge says its about 10 degrees, so, that seems about right for Valley Forge."

Carolyn could not think of Private Allen, Valley Forge, or the cold outside. Only that her mother had singled her out!

'What about my sisters?' she thought but didn't dare say aloud. 'They're in the DAR, and I've heard them brag about it—all the time! What about them?'

Like anyone who is the only one selected for reprimand, it's never fair. She wanted to scream at her mother that her DAR sisters all felt and behaved the same as her.

Carolyn's response to her mother's scolding and her haughty manner—friends did chide her about being 'stuck up'—begged a few questions: Would she climb down from that high horse? Would she outgrow the insecurity that lay behind her need to swagger? Outgrow it before her oversized braggadocio dissuaded any man from taking an interest? It was the latter that finally concerned Abigail Profit.

But she did as her mother bid. She donned the old rags, the blanket, and the scarf.

"Good!" Abigail said. "Now get out there and do your duty for God and country, Private Profit!"

Her mother's apparent attempt at humor did not amuse Carolyn, but the girl took pride in lasting a bit more than two hours in the knee-deep snow outside without benefit of fire or shelter. When she came back into the kitchen after shaking the snow from her feet and legs, her mother had drawn a hot tub. That cramped, tin, oversize bucket had never felt so good.

Later, when her father returned from the manufactory, Abigail told him of their daughter's penance. He said nothing to her until bedtime. When she bent to kiss him good night, he looked up and said, "Good going, Private Profit."

§

By the time of the horse-trough incident and Conrad's unexpected appearance and courtship overture, the conversation about boasting and the questions raised thereby, plus conversations with or about Conrad Bauer, caused Abigail to realize something about her daughter that had gone unnoticed: Carolyn had become either stubborn or a rebel.

That stubbornness, or rebelliousness, if that's truly what it was, seemed odd to Abigail considering the Profits' conscious efforts to control their daughters' maturation. It shouldn't have. After all, they had three married daughters. Had Abigail and Sam not learned something of rebellion from them? Nonetheless, for a reason or reasons that Abigail could not discern at once, Carolyn the 'rebel' seemed different, which quietly pleased her.

There was another aspect of the matter to consider as well, perhaps *not* so pleasing. The suddenness of Abigail's discovery of Carolyn's rebelliousness had refocused her mind on a question she had struggled to avoid for years: Had she and Sam been overly protective? She didn't care for the answer, but neither could she deny its truth: they had.

Abigail slapped her forehead with the heel of her hand, as though knocking some sense into her head. Well intentioned as she and Sam believed it to be, their method of parenting had reached a new and unanticipated level of sheer ineffectiveness with Carolyn: their 'children' were no longer children. Of course, that reality, a normal evolution, had been clear for any outsider to see for several years, but it had never struck a chord with Abigail as it did that fateful day, two days before the Fourth. How Sam would react to Abigail's news remained to unclear. In a pinch, she thought cunningly, she could always blame everything on Ezra Allen.

§

The girls had all tried in school to uncover the role Ezra Allen played in securing American independence. They found his name on the Valley Forge muster sheets, but that was the extent of it. Beyond that, they got only a general sense of the army's experience that winter, but it wasn't what they expected.

The outnumbered Continental Army under General Washington's command tried, and failed, to protect Philadelphia from the British. Washington then had to balance the Continental Congress's wish for some type of winter campaign to dislodge the British from the capital against the needs of his weary and poorly supplied army.

In December 1777, he decided on a strategic retreat to Valley Forge. From this location, 20 miles northwest of Philadelphia, the army was close enough to maintain pressure on the British yet far enough away to prevent a surprise attack. Valley Forge had another often-overlooked advantage.

There, the girls had learned through diligent searching, Washington's men were not the helpless victims of a harsh winter, the generally accepted version of Valley Forge. Rather than wait for deliverance, the army located supplies, built log cabins, constructed makeshift clothing and gear, and cooked subsistence meals of their own concoction. Disease, not cold or starvation, was the true scourge of the camp. Despite the obvious hardships, or perhaps because of them, Washington used the winter to build his army into a better fighting force.

"I think Ezra Allen was one of those who died of disease," Carolyn announced with finality to her mother one day after their heated discussion about Carolyn's snootiness.

Abigail smiled and nodded wordlessly. Apparently, Carolyn's conclusion ended all curiosity among the Profits about their not-so-famous revolutionary patron.

13

THE 'BAUER PERSON'

The Profit home was remarkably unpretentious. Its white clapboard, balloon-frame style beneath a steeply pitched roof—common in western towns, particularly those subject to heavy snowfalls—differed little from other residences in town, despite Sam Profit's comparative wealth.

The need in the West for speed and ease of construction advantaged the balloon-frame design over those of traditional brick, stone, and mortar more typical of the East. Houses of long, continuous, lightweight wooden studs (2x4) that supported siding and walls reduced the cost, the amount of labor, and construction skills. One or two people could quickly put up such a house. Towns like Griggs appeared to rise overnight.

But cheap, light, and quick equaled flimsy. To some observers, balloon-frame houses appeared so fragile they might blow away or burst at any moment. A house fire offered no mercy whatsoever.

The Profit property included more acres than was typical in Griggs, but there was little else to suggest the kind of upper-crust appearance a successful manufacturer with a large payroll might wish to show.

Inside the home, a hall extended from the front entrance to the rear door, separating rooms, left and right. Halfway along its length the hallway was wide enough to support a flight of narrow stairs to the second floor.

Nearest the front entrance—keeping to the left-right arrangement of rooms—family and visitors could choose either a casual living room on one side or a more formal parlor on the other. They could join others in one room or escape from them in the other, a not uncommon occurrence.

Next came a dining room on the left side, and behind it a kitchen where the washing of bodies and clothes also took place. Sam and Abigail's bedroom stood across the hall. Upstairs, before two of them married, the young Profits occupied two bedrooms.

There was no 'indoor plumbing'; matters thereof were the responsibility of an outhouse. Periodically, someone had to empty and burn what lay beneath a solid oak bench with three oval-shaped, carefully crafted, and sanded holes, one for children and a pair for adults should they choose simultaneous occupation.

§

The Profit family sat for supper.

"Why are we talking about this 'Bauer' person? Sounds German. And a 'coal man,' you say? Have you met his people, Carolyn?"

The way he said, 'person,' 'coal man,' and 'his people' strongly suggested disapproval and prejudice. Sam's characterizations elicited disapproving glances from Abigail.

"It *is* German, Father ... What you said is so dismissive. He worked for you for a short time. Did you know that?"

Sam shrugged. "No, I didn't, but I can't keep track of everyone. I have a bookkeeper for that. Is there something going on I don't know about?"

Silence, then ...

"He's invited Carolyn to the picnic on the Fourth," Abigail offered.

"I see," Sam replied. His face now showed a genuine interest.

"Well, there's more you should know about him, Father. Conrad, his mother, and two sisters emigrated after the father in Germany died. I think that's just an amazing thing to do. Conrad was only eleven. He said he was seasick the whole voyage. And, no, I have not met the family—yet."

"Well, young lady, wouldn't meeting them be important? I've heard of a shoe repairman in town named 'Bauer.' They say he can make a mean pair of boots. Is that the same family?"

"Yes."

"Why haven't you brought this young man to me? You do understand that's the way it works, don't you?"

"Of course, Father. That was my intention. He's very shy. Just ask Mother."

Sam Profit turned to his wife whose expression and shrug confirmed Carolyn's opinion.

"Guess what, Sam."

Abigail decided the subject needed changing.

"I can't possibly," he said irritably.

"He called me, 'Ma'am'! More than once."

Carolyn started to laugh but stopped at once when subjected to her father's glare.

"No! He didn't! Really? But you set him straight, right?"

"Yes, Father, she certainly did!" Carolyn interrupted. "It was so unfair!" And she began to tear up.

"You keep a civil tongue in your head, young lady," Sam Profit warned. "You may not be a girl any longer, but that does not mean you are free to disrespect your mother or me. Is that clear?"

Carolyn looked to refocus the discussion on Conrad. Her mother saw her distress and offered cooperation.

"I thought I was very pleasant with him," Abigail said, referring to the earlier discussion of 'Ma'am.'

"Conrad didn't know better, Mother. He had just met you and was trying to be polite. Besides, he was my guest!"

"Well, I'm sure he learned his lesson," Samuel said. It was a familiar signal known to everyone that they should move on to something else.

Still, Carolyn continued to pout.

14

THE FOURTH

"Carolyn, is that Conrad I see coming up the lane?"

It was the Fourth, at last, and Conrad carried a small wooden box as he approached the Profit home.

Presumably, that box held his contribution to the picnic, which would follow the parade. His proposal for their picnic, which he planned to present to Carolyn, included a semi-private spot on the bank of Buffalo Creek. He understood intuitively that Carolyn's father might have something to say about that.

"Hello, Mrs. Profit," Conrad said as he stood before the front door. "I wish you a Glorious Fourth of July. Three cheers for Independence! Is Carolyn available?"

"Come in, Conrad. I think Mr. Profit would like to speak to you in the living room. Carolyn is still dressing upstairs."

Conrad blanched, but he knew meeting Carolyn's father was necessary. He knew that dreaded day would have to come, and now it had. First, however, while standing in the hallway, Conrad awkwardly presented the box to Abigail.

"It's something for the Profit family from the Bauer family," he explained.

"Why, thank you, Conrad."

"My mother thought you might like to taste some genuine strudel. It's a dessert—*Apfelstrudel*. But you can eat it any time. She also wrote out the recipe—in case you'd like to make it yourself one day."

"How thoughtful of your mother, Conrad. Please express our thanks. What is her name, please?"

"Anna Maria." There is a smaller amount of strudel in the box for our picnic. So, if you take out the larger pieces, below the separator, I'll keep the top ones for Carolyn and me."

"Mr. Profit is waiting."

She made him sound like a hangman. Conrad smiled anyway and walked into the living room.

"Come in, son, come in," Sam said, as he rose and pointed to a chair in the corner of the room.

"Should I sit, sir?"

"Yes, unless you are planning on leaving."

Conrad took that as a hint that perhaps he should leave, the quicker the better, but he sat as directed instead. Sam broke the awkward silence.

"Carolyn said you once worked for me. In what department?"

"Assembly, sir."

"Hmmm ... I usually recognize my employees."

"I'm sorry we never ran into each other, when I work for someone, I work for them."

"I see. Very commendable. But I think we should talk about something else. I'm told you seek my permission to court Carolyn."

"Yes sir."

"Are you in love with Carolyn?"

Profit's abrupt question took Conrad by surprise. He wasn't sure about love, but he thought he should be in love, and he sensed Carolyn's father expected it of him.

"Yes sir, I believe I am."

"You *believe* you are?" Sam practically shouted.

"I *am*, sir," Conrad tried to sound more convincing.

Sam looked at him in a manner strongly suggesting disbelief.

"Then why have you waited until now to reveal this 'love'?"

Profit's questions were forcing him to think faster than was comfortable. He struggled.

"I needed to establish myself, sir, you know, to find a steady way to support myself ... and a wife," he quickly added.

Conrad's answer put Sam on the defensive, and he didn't like it.

"So, what do you have to offer my daughter? Do you earn enough to support her *if* I give permission?"

Now, Conrad sensed he had the upper hand.

"If you will forgive me, Mr. Profit, I believe I have as much to offer Carolyn as you had Mrs. Profit. Respectfully."

Faint tittering filtered down from upstairs.

"One more sound from up there and no one, and I mean *no one*, is going to a parade or a picnic. I'm still the father in this family!" he bellowed, looking up. Then he turned back to Conrad, who seemed to have shrunk.

"Well, you've got guts young man, coming at me like that. But you haven't answered my question."

"I work for the coal dealership in Griggs, Mr. Profit. You are one of my customers, my most esteemed one."

"Humph," Profit muttered, but he was starting to like Conrad's combativeness.

"The bank manager told me that soon I will have enough collateral for a loan to buy out Mr. Belcher."

Profit contemplated what he'd just heard for a good ten to fifteen seconds, twiddling his thumbs between his knees.

"Carolyn?"

He looked up and shouted her name loud enough to be heard.

"Yes?" her muffled voice answered.

"You better come down here. You have a visitor."

"Yes, Father. Coming!"

Seconds later an out-of-breath and flushed Carolyn appeared at the door. Conrad rose but Sam did not.

"Did you know this young man … What's your name, again?"

For the moment, Profit ignored Conrad's name and his knowledge about what he had offered Abigail, which he did not deny, and which he must have heard from his daughter.

"Conrad, sir. Conrad Bauer."

"Carolyn, did you know that Conrad here loves you? Said he does."

Carolyn wore a lovely, printed frock, one her mother had sewn for her. It featured reds, whites, and blues in mixed, patriotic patterns, quite striking for the time.

She took the chair next to Conrad, opposite and across the room from her father. On this 'Independence' Day, she embodied its symbolism.

"Yes, Father," she blushed, glancing back and forth between Conrad and Sam.

"'Yes,' he said it, or 'yes,' you know?"

"I know ... now."

"What do you plan to do with this knowledge?"

She looked at Conrad for help. He screwed up his courage.

"If I may, Mr. Profit, I intend to ask for her hand," he said without the level of conviction to satisfy a prospective bride.

"Son," he oozed smugly, "it seems you just did."

That smugness lasted only so long as he'd said it.

"Oh, Father!" she wailed, half crying, half shrieking, "now you've gone and ruined everything! No girl wants to receive a proposal in front of her father!" she shouted at him and ran in tears for the hall and stairs. Conrad glared at Profit and jumped up after her.

Abigail heard the ruckus from in the kitchen.

"What's going on, Sam?" she said, now standing at the doorway. It was less a question than a demand.

"Puppy love, Abigail, puppy love in all its nonsensical drama," he repeated sarcastically, which, of course he shouldn't have. As if to emphasize his exasperation, he threw up both arms.

"Carolyn's your daughter, Sam! She's nearly thirty. It's not 'puppy love' at that age. I'm surprised at you. Go up there and apologize. Comfort her."

"Conrad's gone up to do the comforting," Sam said, excusing himself. He wasn't about to back down completely. "When she comes back down, I will make amends."

Then, a change of tone.

"You know, Abigail," he said without looking directly at her, as though he was searching for the right words, "that boyfriend of hers stood right up to me. She could do worse."

He needed to stop digging himself further into that hole.

"Well, he's not a 'boyfriend' any longer. Let this be a lesson to you, Sam Profit. Have a little faith in your daughter."

Then Abigail said something she shouldn't have.

"You know, Sam, I don't remember my father telling *me* that you stood equally strong when you went through what you put Conrad through. But that doesn't mean I don't love you very, very much … sometimes."

15   AN ANNOUNCEMENT

Carolyn and Conrad descended to the hall and into the living room. By then, Sam Profit had marshaled the courage needed to offer a proper apology. Carolyn accepted it with a hug and more tears; she knew how hard that come down had been for him. Abigail smiled and rubbed her husband's shoulder in support.

§

As they watched the parade, Abigail and Sam discussed what had happened in their living room earlier in the day. Then, Sam changed the subject.
"Do you think the Bauers are here, Abigail?"

"Probably, but let's concentrate on the parade and the meaning of this day, not on people we don't know."

But Sam couldn't let it go. To his wife, he seemed incorrigible.

"A shoemaker and a coal man, Abigail? Really?"

"Okay! Stop right there, Mr. Profit! Snooty comments—maybe I should call them prejudices—don't become you. What and who were you when I agreed to marry? That shouldn't take you long to answer. But if you don't have an answer, I can help. You were struggling, tinkering with things only you understood, an unfulfilled project with no prospects. But I saw something in you, and you did, too! I see in Conrad the same confidence you had in yourself. Our daughter sees it just as I did in you."

He leaned into her and kissed her forehead. It was a kind of messaging between them, a code. Something they had learned to rely on over many years. On most of those occasions, words would have been superfluous.

§

On their way to the parade, Conrad stopped occasionally on a grassy hillside to pick some small flowers. He also gathered a few stalks of Queen Anne's Lace and tied then into a bundle with the stem of a dandelion. Carolyn watched this with bemusement. Conrad looked at her and smiled.

Once they topped the small hill, for hills in that part of North Dakota were not high, the sight of the town caused them to gasp. Dozens of covered wagons heading for the celebration filled the roads. They came from several nearby towns: Laurel, Metamora, Dublin, and Hanen's Woods.

Many arrived early and staked out their tents two blocks north of Main Street where there were fewer houses and more open space.

People milled about everywhere. Excitement filled the air. The Fourth of July offered the only opportunity people had to get together and really celebrate each year; at Christmastime blowing and drifting snow kept them inside. On Main Street they found a place to stand relatively free of people.

"Conrad?"

"Yes, Carolyn."

"Did the Germans have anything like our Fourth?"

He thought for a moment.

"*Oktoberfest*, maybe. I was really too young to know."

"Were there fireworks?"

"I don't think so. It was intended for drinking as much beer as you could in the shortest amount of time."

"There's also Mardi Gras for the Catholics. More drinking. You're not Catholic, are you?"

"Heavens no! I've never tried beer. Have you?"

He turned a bit crimson.

"Yes," he said weakly.

Then, he recovered.

"Peter and Mother like it."

"And you don't?"

He shrugged.

"Carolyn?"

"Yes."

"I'd like to change the subject."

Conrad's interrogation by Sam had emboldened him. Now, it seemed, he had decided he loved Carolyn enough to … Her answer interrupted his thinking about what he would say next.

"Okay," she agreed to changing the subject.

Carolyn knew what was coming, but she wasn't going to deny him his moment as her father had.

Conrad, on the other hand, felt a bit trapped. He liked Carolyn, no doubt of that, but he truly wasn't sure about 'love.' Sam Profit, he felt, had practically forced him—trapped him—into proposing, indeed had done it *for* him. He concluded he must go ahead.

"Carolyn, I'd like you to consider becoming my wife."

She gave him a look of disappointment.

"Can't you rephrase that, Conrad? Do you want to marry me, or am I merely to consider it?"

"Oh, *verdammt*," he muttered so she wouldn't hear. "Of course, I want to marry you! I don't have a proper ring, but I will. I wove this one with those flowers I've been picking. May I put it on your finger? Maybe you should hold the rest of the 'bouquet' with your right hand."

Before he could retrieve the 'ring' from a pocket, Carolyn dropped the 'flowers,' threw her harms around him, and kissed him fully on the lips. When she had finished, he pulled slightly back and looked around.

Satisfied no one seemed interested in them, he drew her close enough to kiss her cheek and lips, where he lingered. He felt the warmth and softness of her body, and it embarrassed him to discover his body responding to a woman in a manner not unfamiliar to him when alone. Carolyn felt it, too, and gently pressed her hips into his.

The moment passed, though in time much longer than a 'moment,' leaving the pair bathed in perspiration and breathing rapidly. Carolyn, embarrassed by what had just happened, needed to change the subject. Perhaps she thought that doing so would expunge what had happened and restore her innocence.

"Don't you think we should tell Mother and Father? And your mother? I'd love to meet her, Conrad."

"You mean …"

She gave him a look.

"No! Dummy! I mean about our engagement.

His suggestion of something other than their engagement was the first time she'd considered the truth of what had just happened, and it caused her to blush.

"Yes, of course, we should tell them … about our being engaged.

Their conversation returned to the prosaic.

"Mother and Father planned to go to the picnic grounds with my unmarried sister. They'll have fireworks there after dusk. We could look there. We'll have to walk back home. Did your mother to attend the picnic?"

"No, she's a bit too old. My sisters planned to go with their husbands. I'm not sure about my brother. He lives alone, now. He used to share the family place."

"Conrad, I don't even know the names of your family."

"Today is probably not the right occasion to meet them, but I want to arrange something soon."

"Tell me their names, Conrad. Your sisters were ahead of us in school, so I didn't know them. I've seen your brother's shop."

"Peter is the oldest; he's the shoemaker. Marta and Louise are my big sisters. Mother is Anna Maria."

"My, what a beautiful name!"

"I'm what the farmers would call the 'runt of the litter.'"

Carolyn threw her head back in laughter.

§

Before returning to the Profit place to announce their engagement, the newly betrothed couple stopped to watch a bit of the parade. Typical for a rural town in 1899, it consisted mostly of horse-drawn, flatbed wagons, their sides festooned with red, white, and blue bunting.

A combination of the local police and men dressed in 'Revolutionary' getup walked alongside the wagons on either side.

These 'patriotic' flatbeds, practically every other display in the procession, invariably featured a young or not-so-young 'Lady Liberty' dressed in layers of sheer, flowing white cloth.

Occasionally, other themes rolled into view. Patriotism had many guises. The fire department, for instance, sponsored a float of its men fighting a mock housefire. Some along the street questioned its appropriateness. Another float offered parade watchers a classroom. A teacher dressed in a white neck-high blouse and an ankle-length black skirt stood with a pointer at a blackboard; a 'roomful' of students appeared to be listening to every word. Some along the street questioned its realism. And, of course, on one flatbed after another, wheat farmers stood or sat next to sacks of the life-giving grain. No one questioned their appropriateness or realism.

Realism existed elsewhere. The stench of horse manure left behind by the poor beasts doing all the pulling was real enough. A thermometer near the entrance of the mercantile building read 93°. A perfect storm.

16   ANNA MARIA

A week after the holiday festivities, Conrad presented Carolyn to his mother. Anna Maria had been just as surprised as the Profits with the news of her son's engagement to a woman she'd never met. When she learned of his involvement with Carolyn, she scolded him and insisted on meeting the young woman ... at once. She prepared more *Apfelstrudel* for the occasion.

"I'm pleased to meet you, Miss Profit. Conrad has told us so much about you," Anna Maria intoned in the sweetest vice she could muster as the couple came into the living room. The second part of her greeting was untrue.

"I'm so happy to know you, Mrs. Bauer."

"Please," Anna Maria said, "let's sit and have some *Apfelstrudel*. Do you drink tea or coffee, Miss Profit?"

"Neither, thank you. A glass of water would be fine. And do call me Carolyn."

When the party of three had finished the *Apfelstrudel*, Anna Maria invited Carolyn into her bedroom. The invitation briefly puzzled Carolyn, but Conrad encouraged her to go.

"I have some inexpensive family jewelry that I managed to bring over with me," Anna Maria explained. "I sewed all of it into my clothing so that the customs officials would not find it. I wanted to give the pieces to my children when they married. I did the same for my daughters when they married ...

"Peter, I'm afraid, has passed the age to find a suitable partner and never showed an interest doing so ...

"So, I have chosen this necklace for you. My hope is that you will wear it at your wedding. I know it isn't worth very much—my family in Germany was not wealthy—but as it passed to me from my mother and to her from my grandmother, it represents not simply a family connection, a family history, but I also attach much sentimental value to it."

Carolyn's eyes turned misty as she accepted the necklace. It appeared to be attractive costume stones—oranges, greens, and yellows set in intricately designed gold plating.

"Oh, it's beautiful!" Carolyn gushed. It will mean so much to me, as you explained where it comes from. May I give you a small kiss?"

Anna Maria gave a small laugh. "Of course, if it pleases you to do so."

Carolyn kissed Anna Maria's cheek and the pair rose from the bed on which they had been sitting to rejoin

Conrad. After a respectable period of small talk, the young couple rose and said goodbye to Anna Maria.

Carolyn promised to show him the necklace when they arrived. Abigail thought it 'lovely' and 'very touching,' but Conrad hadn't much to say. Doubtless, he was thinking of its family devolution and the way in which his mother hid it from the American authorities, which she had proudly told the family many times. He merely said he hoped she'd wear it for their wedding. His unenthusiastic endorsement puzzled and disappointed Carolyn.

How could it have been otherwise? Carolyn had no feeling for or experience in her life to understand what it meant to Anna Maria to give up everything except her children and some unmarketable baubles whose only value lay in their history, and on top of that go to the lengths she did to make sure she could trust them to another generation.

Mistake or no, Carolyn couldn't let his clear indifference go without explanation.

"Try to put yourself in her place, as difficult as that is. Her children, the clothes on her back, and those seemingly cheap heirlooms were all she had when we arrived in America ...

"She got me through the health examination through sheer insistence, and she protected those seemingly cheap heirlooms from the clutches of customs officials. Those men would have kept them for themselves ...

"That's what I was thinking about when you showed it to your mother. I'm sorry. I wasn't thinking in the moment. I should have been more attentive to what the necklace meant to you. I agree. It was a touching thing for her to do. She obviously liked you, which is very easy to do!"

He put his arm around her shoulders and gently kissed her cheek.

17 BISMARCK

"Carolyn," her mother said, far too casually to Carolyn's liking, "you must allow me to be in charge of your wedding. I know times are changing, but I believe that's still a mother's prerogative. Besides, I've been looking forward to it since the day you were born!"

Carolyn had to take her mother's 'prerogative' seriously, and she responded with cautious civility. She and Conrad wanted a wedding of their own doing. Funny, she thought. Abigail seemed oddly insistent—out of character. She also wondered if her mother had been just as insistent with her married sisters, and she made a mental note to ask them.

"Yes, Mother, but you must agree to certain of our ideas, Conrad's and mine. Do you think you can agree to that?"

"Of course, Dear."

Carolyn understood tradition, and she didn't want to be unpleasant. But she also wanted this to be the last time they'd speak of how much responsibility for the wedding they'd share with Abigail.

Perhaps the couple's insistence on a degree independence was best exemplified by the choice of the date. It was to be June! Carolyn and Conrad thought themselves quite clever in deliberately choosing both a pagan and a Christian month for their nuptials.

The word 'June' originated with *Juno*, the Roman goddess of marriage. June, as it applied to Christianity, fell well after Lent, an event that signaled the onset of warmer weather. And summer was of great interest in North Dakota! So, it would be Tuesday, June 12, at 10 A.M.

When Sam Profit—a religious man when it suited him and certainly never a pagan—When Sam Profit listened to their reasoning, he thought them a bit too clever and, being true to himself if not diplomatic, said so.

§

The Edwardian era wedding changed the Victorian version only marginably; Carolyn and Conrad's nuptials came under the sway of both. Many Edwardian era wedding dresses kept some Victorian qualities: silk, lace, and other luxurious fabrics. But Edwardian dresses flowed with a greater softness.

For her wedding, Carolyn had decided—under her mother's watchful eye and threatened veto—to wear low-heeled shoes, a traditional white dress of silk, linen, and lace with no train and no veil. Jewelry she restricted to the necklace from Anna Maria.

Months before the event, Carolyn, her mother, and Katherine, who joined them to give a third opinion on the best choice of a dress, took the train to Bismarck to shop for wedding apparel. With Sam's family in Bismarck spending more of his money than he might have wished, he and Conrad found time to chat.

Sam Profit was not a miser in all things related to money, but he did view the spree in Bismarck as far less important an indulgence than something of greater permanence—something in the way of security for his daughter. His family's having fun with the outing in Bismarck was something that needed doing, but he looked on his family responsibilities as he did his business. Some things were better investments than others.

Sam and Abigail had agreed before Bismarck that their gift to the newlyweds would be a home. To that end, Sam and Abigail were prepared to offer a sizeable down payment, subject to a choice of home satisfactory to the couple.

"I wish to be clear about this Conrad. You and Carolyn will handle the mortgage. Is that understood? Do you agree? Can you manage it?"

"My answer is 'yes' to all three, sir. But most of all I want to thank you. Carolyn is so fortunate to have parents like you and Mrs. Profit."

"Humph," Profit muttered. Believing himself above sentimentality, in other words, tough, he did not suffer compliments easily. He decided to adjust the subject of their conversation, a choice he came to understand had been a colossal mistake.

"And what will your family be giving the bride and groom?"

Doubtless, he asked this in full knowledge that Conrad's mother could not possibly top his and Abigail's gift.

"Mother has already given Carolyn a small gift, a family heirloom, a necklace. It hasn't much monetary value, certainly nothing like a house. But she brought it here just for this purpose by hiding it from customs officials at Castle Garden. It truly came from her heart."

Sam Profit couldn't decide whether Conrad was being impertinent or sentimental. For once, he made the correct choice. He simply nodded his acknowledgement. He knew the young man in front of him had bested him, and he knew Carolyn had made a wise choice.

§

The carefree Bismarck adventure had to end, and it did. Abigail felt young and gay again in the presence of the girls and her command of another wedding! She loved her husband very much, but he could be very stifling—an ol' fuddy-duddy is how she put it—when it came to her desire to do things unrelated to his interests.

"We had a grand time in the *big* city, Father," Carolyn cried happily as she kissed her father. She drew out the word 'big' for emphasis. "I'm sure Mother told you all about it. Shopping, restaurants ... everything! Now look at this, Father." She held out her left hand for him to admire. "I don't think you've seen Conrad's ring."

As usual, Sam wondered how a coal man could afford such a piece. What he saw was not simply a gold ring but a moderately-sized diamond solitaire in a high, gold-pronged setting called a Tiffany.

"It's as spectacular as my daughter," he exclaimed and kissed Carolyn's cheek.

18 CONFESSION

A few days shy of a month following the Bismarck caper, Carolyn stood on a small platform in the bedroom she used to share with Phyllis. The prospective bride, reduced that morning to a sort of mannequin, issued directions to Katherine and Abigail who circled the grown-up, real-life doll with pins clenched between teeth and lips. They consulted occasionally, sometimes frantically, all the while adjusting and readjusting every detail of the dress.

Sam knocked on the bedroom door.

"Just a minute, Father," Carolyn shouted over the din of buzzing females.

Finally, they allowed him entry. Abigail and Katherine stood aside with Sam to admire Carolyn and their handiwork.

But Carolyn wasn't standing still. She tugged up her skirts and fell into her father's arms.

"Oh, Father, the dress is so beautiful, so perfect. It's everything I dreamed of having for that day."

"And you, My Dear, are the picture of beauty and perfection. Conrad is a lucky guy. Do you think he'll show up? ... Just kidding."

"You better be kidding, Sam Profit," his wife threatened, "or I'll march right downstairs and get that roller we've been using for the pie dough and crown your head!

"I hope you didn't spend a fortune on the dress, Father," even though she knew he had ... "but on the other hand, I hope you did!"

That broke the seriousness of the moment, and everyone laughed.

§

"Carolyn," her mother said, as the bride-to-be and Katherine were preparing supper one evening shortly before the wedding. "I need to talk to you about the wedding. Will you have a few minutes after we've cleared and washed the dishes?"

"Yes, of course, Mother." But there was a seriousness in her mother's tone that struck Carolyn as unusual to any discussion of the wedding.

"Have you been gaining weight, My Dear? Abigail began after the washing up. "I noticed when we adjusted your dress that your waistline did not match the measurements we took when we picked out the dress. Your waistline is thicker now, and your breasts have grown."

"Really?"

"Is there anything you want to tell me about Conrad and you, something I don't know, but, as your mother, I should? Have you been sick?"

Carolyn, who sat on the living room divan, bent over and, with her elbows on her thighs, put her face between her hands and began to sob.

"How many periods have you missed, darling? ... Had they been regular?"

Carolyn raised her head.

"Three. Very regular. My next one should have been now. I have been sick ... once."

"So, you may be twelve weeks."

"Yes, twelve weeks. I remember when it happened because it was the only time."

"Was it Conrad?"

"Of course, Mother! I'm not that kind of girl!"

"May I ask how it happened, and where? Whose bed did you use?"

"No! You may not ask!"

"You must tell me. You must trust me. I would never say or do anything to hurt you, Carolyn."

"Oh, Mother, it's so embarrassing!" and she sobbed louder.

"Carolyn? I'm waiting, and neither of us is going anywhere until you tell me what happened."

"Promise me you won't punish Conrad."

"I am not going to punish either of you. I understand these things can and do happen."

"Well, to answer your last question, it wasn't a bed, Mother. We were walking around town, which we do a lot, and found ourselves behind the blacksmith shop. When we were sure no one was around, we just started kissing and touching each other."

"Where?"

"Mother! ... You know. Please don't make me say it."

"Say it, Carolyn!"

"Well, I could feel his 'member' against my leg and my, you know."

"Yes, yes. Go on."

"So, we were still kissing a lot, pushing against each other, and I wanted to know what it was like, what it felt like to hold it, so I unbuttoned is trousers, and his fornicating thing sprang out. So, I held it and moved my hand back and forth. It felt good. I know it shouldn't have, but it did. Then, I noticed I became wet inside. It was something like my period, except it wasn't."

"And?"

"Please don't hate me for this, Mother. But I'm going to tell you something that you should never hear from a daughter."

"Carolyn, you are my precious child. I could never hate you, but you must tell me what Conrad did. He needs to be accountable."

"Mother! It wasn't Conrad. Please, don't blame him. It was me! I wanted him *soo* much!"

"What do you mean, it was you?"

"I let go of his 'thing' and pulled up my skirt. I was against the shop wall. I didn't have on underpants because of using the outhouse. I don't know how I knew the next part; it just seemed intuitive. Anyway, I told him to lift my legs and put them around his waist ..."

"Carolyn!"

"... Put my legs around his waist, which he did. He's very strong; he could hold me up the whole time. I pushed my bottom as close to him as I could and then put his thing into my thing. I suppose intuition made us both move against each other—it seemed so natural—for about a minute until I heard him gasp several times. After another minute, it seemed, he put me down ...

"We kept kissing and breathing hard. There! I said it! And I'm so ashamed in telling you about it, but I'm not ashamed of doing what I did! I love him so much, Mother." With that, she burst into tears.

"Honey, you can never keep a man if you make him marry you because you're carrying his child."

"That's not what happened. He knows about the baby. He's happy with me and my having his child. And I'm so happy to be carrying his child. It means something of him is always with me, especially when we're apart."

"Oh, dear. What can I say? ... Well, I'll begin here. First, I'm glad you told me everything that happened. Second, I want both to slap you and hug you. Third, the wedding is very soon, so we can credibly explain away a few weeks as a premature birth. Do you understand?"

"Yes, I think so."

"You must not tell your father. He won't believe you, and he'll go after Conrad and do God knows what to him. Understood?"

"Yes."

"Please say, 'I understand.'"

"Yes, Mother, I understand."

"Does Katherine know."

"No, of course not."

"No one is to know. Just the three of us. But as soon as you are married, I want to take you to the doctor. That baby needs caring for, as do you …

"Now, I want you to take me to Conrad. I need to be sure he understands his new responsibility."

§

The next day Abigail and Carolyn took the buggy to Belcher Coal. Conrad saw the buggy coming and guessed, correctly, that he was about to face Abigail's wrath. Mr. Belcher wasn't there, as usual, so, Conrad had no difficulty making time for the visitors.

Carolyn reined in the horse, stepped down, and ran to Conrad. He saw her distress and put his arms around her. Abigail dismounted and strode menacingly toward Conrad before Carolyn could explain to him the reason for their visit.

"Hello, Mrs. Profit," he said, hoping to diffuse what it appeared would be a difficult confrontation. Abigail did not disappoint.

"Young man! she practically shouted. "Has Carolyn told you she is with child and you are the father?"

"Yes ... Mrs. Profit." He nearly called her, 'Ma'am.'

"Well, what do you intend to do about it? Are you going to marry Carolyn? Be a responsible father to the child you are bringing into this world?"

Conrad waited to speak, making sure he chose his words carefully.

"In one month, Mrs. Profit, I am marrying Carolyn. It will be the happiest day of my life. Then, eight months later we, Carolyn and I, will become the parents of a wonderful girl or boy, and you will be that wonderful child's grandmother. That will be the second happiest day of my life. I can't speak for your days."

He paused again.

"Respectfully, Mrs. Profit, it will be the second happiest day of my life, not because of *your* becoming a grandmother, but because of my becoming the father of a child conceived in love ...

"Respectfully, Mrs. Profit, can you understand my feelings?"

Abigail Profit stared straight at Conrad's eyes.

"Conrad," Abigail said without visible emotion, although her next words failed to disguised a hint of pride, "those words are precisely what I wanted to hear from you ...

"Now, Carolyn, please untie Ellen's reins and drive me home."

"Could you drive yourself, Mother? Now that I'm here, I'd like to spend whatever time Conrad can spare."

"How will you get home?"

"I'll bring her, Mrs. Profit."

"Very well."

Abigail Profit re-mounted the buggy and urged Ellen forward with a *click-click* sucking noise between her tongue and teeth.

19   A WEDDING

Protestantism in Griggs worked on a simple principle: either you were a Lutheran or you were not. Catholics, whose numbers might logically be significant, were a small minority among the religious. Migration to the Dakotas had come principally from northern, Protestant Europe; Catholic Europe lay to the south. No more than a half-dozen 'heretical' families drove their buggies or wagons nine miles west to attend mass at St. Joseph's parish in Upper Creek. This inconvenience, a town without a parish, did not trouble local Protestants in the least.

Carolyn and Conrad's ceremony took place at Faith Lutheran. One could refer to it as 'Carolyn's church' only on paper; the Profit family was not, as the definition of being religious went in that day, a devout lot. This 'neglect' was largely Sam's doing, and everyone in the family went along with the hypocrisy; it was a wedding, after all. So, it followed that bells should peal, and flowers should adorn the church. Inside, the couple signed the parish register.

For her flowers, Carolyn chose white roses and lilies of the valley, a significant assault on Conrad's financial reserves. She wore Anna Maria's necklace, of course. No one had the bad form to hint or inquire of its value, though the most perceptive among them must have seen it wasn't much. None of them could possibly have guessed its true value and the pride with which Carolyn wore it.

The matrons of honor, like Carolyn, wore flat shoes and white dresses. After June 12, those dresses became part of the women's everyday wardrobe.

Conrad wore a traditional black frockcoat, with white, double-breasted waistcoat and grey striped trousers. Peter, his best man wore the same, though more subdued, and both wore a white rose in their lapel. Later, it was safe to say, those outfits did not become part of the men's everyday wardrobe!

Flower girls led the procession down the aisle toward a large canopy of white roses followed by Sam and Carolyn. Three matrons of honor and bridesmaid, Carolyn's sisters, walked behind the bridal couple.

Abigail and friends of the Profit family occupied pews on one side of the aisle; Anna Maria, Conrad's sisters and their families, friends, and those who had worked with Conrad at his various jobs sat opposite.

Carolyn's ring was a plain gold band, engraved inside with the bride and groom's initials and the date.

Sam Profit's prominence throughout the region persuaded The Bismarck *Tribune* to dispatch a reporter to cover the event. His piece, which appeared the next day on the society page, described the bride as 'prominent in society circles for years.' Presumably, he meant DAR circles. Conrad, the *Tribune* continued in a charitable mood, was 'an enterprising young businessman, and a member of the Belcher firm.' The reporter made no mention of Conrad's association with coal.

§

Carolyn and Conrad had discussed their vows beforehand with Pastor William Short who was to perform their ceremony. The clergyman knew Carolyn quite well but Conrad less so. The young man was not so regular a churchgoer as his bride to be. Short explained to the couple but particularly the young man, who he took to be unfamiliar with Lutheran ways, that he went by 'Pastor' rather than 'Reverend' because he, like many Lutheran ministers, saw his work as being that of servant or shepherd for a flock of God's people. In Spanish, he added to reinforce his point, the word pastor meant 'shepherd.'

It was a new century into which this improbable couple were venturing. So, in honor of that once-in-a-lifetime change they explained to Pastor Short their desire to break from the traditional Christian vows and voice commitments of their own. It turned out that Short felt as modern about vows as they.

When the moment came, in keeping with the couple's request but shocking to some of the guests, Pastor Short asked Carolyn and Conrad to face each other and offer their promises.

First, Conrad ...

"In the presence of God and before our family and friends, I, Conrad, take you, Carolyn, to be my wife. All that I am I give to you, and all that I have I share with you. Whatever the future holds, I will love you and stand by you, so long as we both shall live. This is my solemn vow."

Then, Carolyn ...

"I, Carolyn, take you, Conrad, to be my husband and these things I promise you: I will be faithful to you and honest with you; I will respect, trust, help, and care for you; I will share my life with you; I will forgive you as we have been forgiven; and I will try with you

better to understand ourselves, the world, and God; through the best and worst of what is to come, and so long as we live."

Skeptical guests, even those initially shocked, warmed to what they had just seen and heard. Reportedly, there was not a dry eye by the time Carolyn intoned sweetly, 'so long as we live.'

After the ceremony, the couple changed in a church anteroom; Peter stayed behind to pay the 'shepherd.' Guests waited outside with rice, grain—wheat, of course—and birdseed. Little did they know that these symbols of fertility were superfluous at this wedding.

Carolyn and Conrad came out of the church and tried unsuccessfully to run from cascades of those pesky, superfluous symbols that invaded their noses and ears and lodged in their hair—birdseed being the worst offender. Then, trying to pick themselves clean of those tiny 'symbols of fertility,' they walked, the guests falling in behind, to the veteran's hall for a breakfast reception—a 'bounteous collation,' the *Tribune* reported—and an afternoon and early evening of merriment, the latter fueled by all the champagne a successful pump manufacturer could provide.

At dusk, the newlyweds, alone for the first time that day, walked unsteadily toward their new home. If one were to guess how they celebrated that night, for the first time in their lives without the prying eyes and ears of parents and siblings ... Well ... such speculation should not occupy much of one's time or tax one's imagination.

PART IV
ALTERED STATES

20 SIOUX CITY

The Belcher Coal Company never became the Bauer Coal Company. Old Mr. Belcher died, but in a move that stunned Conrad in its duplicity, Belcher changed his Will and left the company to his daughter who, in turn, sold it to a conglomerate in Wyoming associated with mining operations in the Powder River.

"He said nothing to you about his daughter?" an equally disappointed Carolyn asked.

"Never a word. I knew of her, of course, but not that he intended to leave the company to her. I asked if she wanted to sell it to me; I knew she couldn't stick with it, and I was right! But she went behind my back and sold out to that Wyoming outfit. Obviously, they could offer her more."

"There was nothing else you could do, Conrad. Sometimes I think this world has gone mad with greed with all these new inventions—machines. Automobiles, aero planes, electrical this and that. I'm not so sure about so-called progress."

With no prospect in sight in Griggs or nearby towns and cities, Conrad eventually learned of an opportunity in Sioux City, Iowa, and jumped at it. Coal was what Conrad knew. Nothing else.

He and Carolyn sold their home in Griggs, their wedding gift from Sam and Abigail, the one Carolyn hoped to grow old in. With a loan guaranteed by Sam Profit, who saw and appreciated the opportunity that lay before the couple and, it needs to be said, the chance to reap a tidy sum in interest from the arrangement for himself, the Bauers purchased the Sioux City Coal Company. Anna Maria, Peter, Marta, and Louise and their families were all that remained of the Bauers of Griggs.

§

> The Sioux City *Journal*, January 13, 1906—
> Iowa lay is in the tallgrass prairie of the North American Great Plains, historically inhabited by speakers of Siouan languages. Yankton Sioux inhabited the area of the future Sioux City when Spanish and French fur trappers appeared in the 18th century.
> In 1804 the Lewis and Clark Corps of Discovery, dispatched by President Thomas Jefferson, traveled up the Missouri and encamped near what would become Sioux City. A member of the expedition and its only casualty, Sgt. Charles Floyd died of 'bilious colic' (some believe

a burst appendix). The Corps buried him on a bluff overlooking the river.

Development went ahead apace. William Thompson set up a trading post near Floyd's Bluff in 1848 and had early ambitions for founding a city never to be realized. Settlers further upriver, between the Floyd and Big Sioux rivers, met with more success.

The first steamboat arrived in June 1856, loaded with ready-framed, balloon houses and provisions; the first railroad in 1868. James Booge opened the first large-scale meatpacking plant in 1873 and created a demand which ultimately led to the opening in 1884 of the stockyards to hold the doomed, unwitting victims set to satisfy that demand.

The city's building boom included an elevated railroad (the Sioux City Elevated Railway) and early 'skyscrapers.' Street cars, water works, electric lights and other improvements appeared. These changes mirrored the growth that was occurring nationwide, especially in the transition of small pioneer settlements into thriving urban centers.

New factories and homes for an expanding population meant a corresponding demand for coal.

Conrad and Carolyn's decision to uproot from Griggs and move to Sioux City seemed timed to match the moment.

§

The Bauer family of Sioux City, increasingly secure with the growth of the Bauer Coal Company, underwent a 'boom' of its own. Julie Lynn came along as expected in February 1901; John Charles in 1903; and Peter Samuel in 1905.

§

The dynamic and extraordinary growth of the United States, manifested in thousands of communities like Sioux City, turned the country into a world-wide sensation and plunged it, naïveté intact, into the corresponding world of international power politics. The latter included a heavy dose of militarization and the resurrection of mercantilism in the hunt to obtain colonies whose people would labor with little recompense to feed the insatiable demand for increased growth and more territory.

Soon, all too soon, America and its competitors would be beating the drums of all-out war to guarantee once and forever protection of their colonies and racial supremacy. European and Asian powers, including the United States, willingly and thoughtlessly succumbed to colonial competition as if drawn to it by the Lorelei's siren.

21

MODEL T

Samuel Profit turned 72 in 1917, but his youthful energy and outlook betrayed that number. Sam's positivity centered on his making money and finding various ways to fight against aging.

As a result, Sam Profit became a sucker for the 'magical' devices sold through the family's thick, well-worn Sears catalog. Among the gadgetry of particular interest was something described as an electrical belt. Sears guaranteed its curative powers for every ailment, from head colds to unmentionable 'male problems.' Presumably, the belt claimed to supply similar solutions for women.

Profit's pump manufactory continued to thrive. It had netted him far more than his family's needs, past and present, and gave every sign of lasting success. The war in Europe had stimulated wheat cultivation beyond anyone's wildest prediction. If the United States could get it to Europe, the American farmers didn't much care who bought it, Allies or Central Powers ... over there. The boom would come crashing down at war's end, but in 1917, with the United States still on the sidelines but poised to mix it up ... over there, it looked as though hostilities might drag along in stalemate for years. The farmers of North Dakota and the plains stumbled over themselves to reap the millions from what they had sown.

The wheat boom also meant a pump boom. Samuel Profit's products, pumps of all shapes, sizes, and capacities had flooded the western United States and the Canadian plains, with lesser sales in other parts of the two countries. The Profit Pump Manufactory was easily the largest employer in Griggs, and that reputation and service to the community led to Sam's several terms on the city council. The name 'Profit' commanded a predominant, some might argue paternalistic, role in his community and beyond.

§

Sam Profit had been a die-hard tinkerer throughout his life with a great appreciation for metal fabrication of all kinds. As had been the nature of their relationship from the beginning, Abigail mounted a brave and sensible resistance that proved futile. Her historic inability to rein in her husband's curiosity in all things new in the world of mechanics was both a source of resentment and devotion. This aspect of their marriage, doubtless absorbed by

Carolyn, had been a most curious relationship of contrasts that worked.

An example of the Profit's successful disparity occurred in early 1915. It began with a story in the Bismarck newspaper about an 'automobile' race in Chicago two decades earlier. The article reviewed the inventions leading to the successful collaboration in 1892–1893 of two brothers, Charles and Frank Duryea, in creating the first successful American gasoline-powered automobile. It ran on a one-cylinder engine with electrical ignition. Old news in 1915, yes, but news to Sam.

"Listen to this, Abigail," Sam's voice shook with excitement.

> Frank Duryea won the first automobile race in America from Chicago to Evanston, Illinois, and return.

"Just think of it, Abigail!"

'Think of it!' How often Abigail Profit had heard those words, as her husband leaped from one project to another with little regard for reality, a feature of his character she had no difficulty diagnosing. 'Opportunities,' he called them. A 'fool's errand,' she countered.

Sensing disapproval from his wife by her silence, Sam continued reading the article to himself, skimming, or skipping some paragraphs entirely.

> More than 100 companies had organized to manufacture automobiles by 1898.
> The three-horsepower Oldsmobile Runabout, also known as the Curved Dash Olds for its distinctive footboard, became America's best-selling car in 1902, when 2,750 of them were

> sold. Its quantities made it the first mass-produced, gasoline-engine automobile.
>
> The Ford Motor Company sold its first car in July 1903. The company produced 1,700 cars during its first full year of business. Ford turned the automobile from a luxury and a plaything into a necessity by making it cheap, versatile, and easy to maintain.
>
> From 1904 to 1908, an astonishing 241 automobile-manufacturing firms went into business in the United States!

Before he picked up the newspaper that morning, he had been following the progress of the automobile fad. That, and thinking of acquaintances who had bought this marvelous invention, pushed Sam into raising the possibility with Abigail.

"Don't you think we'd enjoy one of those, Abigail?"

"What are you talking about, Sam Profit?"

"You know, an automobile!"

He thought he had the perfect reason (excuse) for such a purchase.

"We could travel to the kids without having to worry about Ellen, her feed, and on and on."

Abigail knew what was coming. He was going to buy a car no matter what she thought about it. She had a counter argument.

"There are such things as trains, Sam. Remember those?"

"But a car would give us more independence."

She couldn't rebut that and sensed defeat.

I'm going to find out if Ford is selling in Bismarck or Fargo, and if not there, Minneapolis.

§

Next week came, and Sam learned something he hadn't expected. He could buy his new Ford Model T via mail order!

"Can you believe it, Abigail? What a country!"

"Humph," she muttered. "How are they getting it here, and what's it going to cost?"

"Just $400, honey. It'll come on the train. What a country!"

She thought of one more argument to discourage him.

"When will it get here?"

"They couldn't say."

A month passed and no automobile. Abigail tried to avoid any mention of the Ford Model T. Then, three months had passed. As her mood lightened, his darkened. He turned morose, and at that point she couldn't stand it.

"Have you made any inquiries, Sam?"

"Yes, of course. No one knows anything, and no one is taking responsibility."

Then, to the exact day six months after he placed the order, he received a telegram from the station master:

> *We have just unloaded one of those automobiles addressed to you for pickup. Please do so at your earliest convenience. We have no space for it.*

Sam let out a whoop! and waved the tele in front of his wife. Then he danced around the kitchen as though he'd just stepped on hot coals.

"Where shall we go first," he asked once he'd calmed down. Phyllis? Elizabeth? Katherine? Carolyn?"

"Who's the eldest?"

"Phyllis it is, then."

"Sam, think about it. Miles City is very far for an automobile trip, don't you think? Maybe you should learn to drive it first! I think seeing Elizabeth and her family in Bloomington makes more sense for a first outing."

"Yes, I suppose you're right," he admitted, his shoulders slumped, a reflection of his disappointment.

Her husband's disillusionment puzzled Abigail. She wondered how something so inconsequential as recognizing he would have to learn to drive if he wanted this automobile could defeat this capable, talented man who had built a profitable business.

22

HERON LAKE

"You goin' down to the lake again, lookin' for those bass you keep talkin' 'bout?"

Wilbur and Nora Moore lived a quarter mile from Heron Lake, southwest of Windom, Minnesota. They had farmed their 35 acres of corn for just as many years. Now, with those acres leased, Nora enjoyed her quilting and visits from grandchildren and Wilbur his favorite bamboo pole and dreams of catching some bass—at least every other day.

Nora's question regarding her husband's plans for the remainder of the day came as they sipped the last of Nora's pot of coffee, which had turned lukewarm. To Wilbur, who was not a man in a hurry for anything, her question was like a broken record, a needle stuck in a grove that produced a scratchy sound, repeated day after day.

It was true. Her sarcastic tone exuded neither love nor a genuine interest in her husband's activities. Its timbre suggested they might have lived together too long.

He gave his wife a look she would not have taken with equanimity if she could have read his face through the whiskers and creases.

"After lunch, I reckon," he answered slowly, as he had after the same tired question day after day.

§

Wilbur Moore inhabited the world required of all dedicated fishermen: patience. Angling, like salvation, came down to time, waiting, of which Wilbur had plenty. He weilded the necessary persistence of a true professional, a steadfastness not unlike that of a small child waiting on Christmas Eve for Santa Claus.

'The God who created those fish could not possibly have created unsuccessful fishermen.'

Wilbur's logic, he was sure, would convince the doubters. Faith and time were on his side.

On the other hand, Nora had good reason to think lightly of her husband's fishing skill. He had proved to be mostly talk and no walk when it came to those bass.

"You mean after your *nap*," she corrected his reference to 'after lunch,' sarcasm oozing all syrupy-like from a sharp tongue.

He tried not to show his irritation. When it came to those bass, their conversation was a road well-trod.

"I reckon."

§

At two o'clock that afternoon, Wilbur and his bamboo pole left for the lake and another mental showdown with those wily bass and, if they weren't on guard, maybe some catfish. He wasn't sure about the latter—Heron Lake was a bass lake—but with Wilbur hope never died. How he loved finishing off those small-mouth bass with some catfish!

Wilbur arrived like clockwork at the rickety wooden dock where he kept his rowboat tied up. He loaded his pole, tackle box and retrieved a bucket from under the dock. That bucket had a dual purpose, one vital—to bail water out of that rowboat, which was nearly as rickety as the dock—and the other … let's just say not so vital—for those bass he looked forward to plopping down in front of Nora to clean and cook. Let 'er make fun of that!

That rowboat wobbled a bit—almost shipping water—as he stepped into it. He sat quickly to lower his center of gravity and pushed off from the dock with one oar—not too hard lest there be no dock when he returned.

§

Days after the station master and a couple of out-of-work men unloaded Sam's purchase and towed it to the Profit place, the excited buyer began a collaboration—a kind of consortium of novice enthusiasts—with the handful of other men in Griggs who owned automobiles.

Eventually, he and the others learned to drive, or so they convinced themselves. After much cajoling and no small amount of wooing, Abigail agreed on some short rides. Eventually, they decided Bloomington, Minnesota, and Elizabeth were not too far for a visit.

Just two months after the train master unloaded Sam's new 'toy,' the Profits were off on a new adventure of some 260-plus miles, part of an increasing number of Americans learning to navigate primitive roads while discovering a new lifestyle. As Sam saw it, the only hiccup might be finding gasoline along the way.

Their route took them across a dirt causeway between fingers of Heron Lake, one of those fingers being Wilbur Moore's favorite. In those early days of motor travel, all of it on dirt roads, no one had given much thought or put much effort into filling the potholes, smoothing the ruts or cutting out protruding tree roots. Most drivers, including Sam, had little or no practice in handling those hurdles. Anyone could have scripted what happened next.

Something on the causeway, a pothole, some ruts or roots—it was never clear what—caused Sam, whose desire for speed exceeded good sense, considering the hazards, to lose control of the Ford. He, Abigail and his Model T of a few weeks plunged full speed into Wilbur Moore's finger and sank at once. Both Profits drowned in their seats before help could arrive.

§

Help began with Wilbur Moore's discovery of the sunken automobile. He thought he'd heard a swishing sound followed by the quacking of ducks and flapping wings as they took flight to escape whatever had disturbed a lazy afternoon.

Then he saw them. Articles of clothing and pieces of wood, broken off by the impact, had floated to the surface, Abigail's bonnet and scarf among them. Hours passed before Wilbur could alert anyone, and more hours before the police and men from the nearest town arrived at the scene with the equipment needed to pull Sam's Model T out of the lake. Wilbur Moore, shaken to the core and empty-handed, walked unsteadily home.

Investigators guessed Sam had confused acceleration with braking, or perhaps potholes had jerked the steering wheel out of his hands. Had an animal on the road had caused the confusion? Had Sam too little practice with braking, accelerating, and steering simultaneously? A combination of all these factors? The local police who conducted a brief investigation into the accident could draw no firm conclusion. Later, the county coroner concluded the impact of the sudden water stop forced driver and passenger into the windscreen, knocking them unconscious.

§

Little wonder. The Model T had three floor pedals. The right pedal was the brake, the center pedal reverse, and the left pedal the clutch. The throttle protruded from the steering column. There was a final hand-foot complication: a multipurpose parking/hand brake, which also played a crucial role in engaging the low and high gears.

To get the Model T moving once started, the driver engaged the low gear by pushing the hand brake from park (fully back) to the 90° middle position (neutral) while depressing the left (clutch) pedal and adjusting the throttle. Once moving, the driver eased off the right pedal (brake), relaxed the left pedal (clutch) all the way up, pushed the hand brake all the way forward to shift into high, and gave it more gas. All this Ford expected the driver to do in deft and simultaneous moves. But in seconds a driver could find his vehicle going too fast. Even at considerably lower speeds, say 25 mph, the Model T reportedly seemed frighteningly fast.

Out there on that barely navigable, dirt causeway everything changed. Imagine Sam, unable to grasp and hold the steering wheel steady, struggling to regain control of his Model T after it began to careen out of control, not knowing which pedal to push and when. What to do? Investigators concluded he didn't know. Confusion reigned.

How might he have kept his Model T out of Heron Lake? If Sam, struggling with the steering wheel, had kept his foot on the right brake pedal, he might have averted disaster. That would have slowed or held the car stationary. Absent that, he would have needed to take several actions simultaneously while he and Abigail became increasingly frightened and hysterical: press the left pedal (clutch) down halfway while pulling the hand brake back to neutral (disengaging the gear) and reduce the throttle. But Sam never reached that point.

Gratuitously, the Ford Motor Company suggested in its user manual that a novice driver 'avoid tight situations until sufficiently practiced.' Sam Profit was not the sort of man to think of himself as either a novice or insufficiently practiced.

§

The Profit daughters and their families, the Bauer extended family, most of Griggs, and politicians from across the Dakotas attended the funeral. The Bismarck *Tribune* reminded residents that Sam Profit had 'built his business while the city was in its infancy.' He was the 'first to provide adequate pumps for Dakota's fields,' a man 'highly esteemed and respected.'

Telegrams and notes of condolence poured in from across the country. There were even telegrams from Henry Ford and President Woodrow Wilson!

But only Sam Profit would have known that none of those accolades belonged to him alone; without Abigail's sacrifice and support there would have been nothing to celebrate.

Carolyn seemed particularly distraught at the funeral service, and she told Conrad and her sister Katherine after the burials that she could not possibly set foot in Griggs again. It would be too strong a reminder of her parents and the memories she had of their lives together.

"I'm not strong enough to bear that, Conrad," she explained in tears. "There's nothing to tie me to the town now that Father and Mother are gone."

Conrad thought that an odd thing to say, considering *his* family still lived there, but he wasn't going to mention it so long as she remained in her present emotional state. To ease her distress, he decided it best they return to

Sioux City as soon as possible. In time, he surmised, she'd change her mind.

23 OF BIRDS & BEES

> *The New York Times*, February 6, 1920—
> In the decade before World War I, powerful socioeconomic and political forces began to coalesce into a growing demand for birth control. State laws had made childhood education compulsory, which removed children from the workforce. When American men went off to fight 'the war to end all wars,' as the Englishman H.G. Wells put it, women filled many of their jobs. Modern life was making it impractical for women to have one child after another after another.
> Bustling prostitution industries sprang up around army bases and seaports during World War I, unleashing an epidemic of venereal disease; condoms became standard issue for sailors. And when the men came home, they weren't

> about to give up the handy access to safe sex to which they'd become accustomed, even though prevention of venereal disease sufficed as the excuse for sales. An organized fight for legalized contraception ensued with Margaret Sanger the face of the movement.

Before Margaret Sanger began to publish her views on family size and the rights of women, Carolyn had reached her own, nearly identical conclusions. She and Conrad decided to avoid another pregnancy after Peter Samuel. Or, to put it more realistically, Conrad would need to avoid impregnating his wife.

When Julie Lynn approached puberty, Carolyn took her aside to explain how her body would change along with her feelings about the other sex. She also emphasized that Julie must be sexually responsible for her sake as well as that of her partner. Men, Carolyn had learned, were less likely than women to behave responsibly.

"When you make friends with a boy, Julie, and I mean a certain kind of friend ..."

Julie cut her off.

"Mother, I know what you mean about a boyfriend. You're going to tell me about making babies. Am I right?"

"Yes, of course."

"Well, my girlfriends talk about that all the time."

"Really?"

That revelation Carolyn found particularly shocking as she'd had no such experience herself.

'It's this damn war,' she mused.

"So, you know about the rhythm method, condoms, diaphragms, spermicides such as ascetic fluids?"

"We're beginning to understand those things."

"Julie, I want to talk to you and the girlfriends you mention. Do your boyfriends understand birth control?"

Julie gave her mother a look of feigned discrimination.

"No. Are you going to talk to John and Peter also?"

Julie thought the mention of her brothers might get her out of a lecture from her mother that she was certain would be embarrassing. Carolyn had a ready reply.

"Your father will speak to the boys, but I want to talk to the boys you are friendly with. Now, listen carefully. This is very important. None of those boys is to come to me until they've first talked to their parents about why I want to speak to them. Do you understand why?"

"Yes, I think so."

"Explain it to me."

"They might think it's none of your business?"

"Exactly."

"So, maybe you shouldn't do it?"

"Don't get smart with me, young lady! Now, if their parents want to talk to them about … you know, about making babies, that's fine with me. But I don't want you around girls or boys who, at your age, don't understand the importance of prevention."

"Mother?"

"Yes, dear?"

"Did *your* mother talk to you about all this?"

By this time, Carolyn had begun to realize she had a very clever daughter, impertinent, yes, and perhaps she'd opened a door to something for which she wasn't prepared and found embarrassing. She decided a short answer—a truthful answer—would avert further discussion.

At the same time, she gave Julie a look that intimated she drop that subject.

"No, Julie."

But as holes go, Carolyn hadn't finished digging hers.

"Mother, was I a premature baby?"

Ouch!

"And who's 'Margaret Sanger'?"

Touché!

Julie's double-barreled questions caught Carolyn completely off guard. She hadn't expected either, so, she took a couple of deep breaths—which did not go unnoticed—before answering.

The first and most difficult question left Carolyn in the uncomfortable position of telling her daughter the truth or lying to her and becoming a hypocrite. So, she equivocated.

"Yes, Julie, you were born early … very early. Everyone worried, but you were strong, and no one could deny you, life."

She squeezed Julie's hand as evidence of her affection. She felt liberated to move on. Julie decided that if her mother believed such a fairy tale, she needn't herself.

"Now," Carolyn continued undeterred by her little lie, "Margaret Sanger is a courageous woman who believes that women must oversee their reproductive lives, whether to conceive or not."

"Doesn't the husband have anything to say about it?"

"Yes, of course. But ultimately it must be the woman's choice."

"That's a radical idea, Mother. Do you know other women who believe that? I can't imagine any man would give in to his wife about whether they should have a child or not."

"Yes, unfortunately, what you say is true. But there are some men ..."

"Father?"

"Yes, of course."

§

"Conrad?"

"Yes, Dear?" he replied after the amount of time a husband usually takes to answer his wife.

"Are you listening to me?" she demanded, clearly put off by his belated response.

"Yes, of course, Dear," this time promptly, as though he couldn't understand her impatience.

"Do you know what your daughter asked me this morning?"

"*My* daughter? Well, let me think ... 'What's for supper?'"

"No! Please, be serious, Conrad ... She wanted to know if she was premature."

"What!"

"Yes, so, you see, nothing to do with supper!" she snapped. "I do wish you'd take what I say a little more seriously now and then."

"I apologize. What did you tell her?"

"I lied, of course, which made me a hypocrite. I had just lectured her about having babies ... how one should take precautions. But it's obvious she has suspicions. She's going to figure it out ... soon enough."

"What will you say then?"

"I'll tell her to ask her father! Then you can be a hypocrite, too."

"I'll say to her just what you did. There's no point in her knowing what we did before we married."

"You know what else she asked, Conrad? She wanted to know about Margaret Sanger."

"What's got her going on all this stuff?"

"She's become a young woman, and she wants to know how to handle that. That's more than either of us did—handle it. We didn't give it one thought before, you know, what happened against the wall of that building ...

"I offered to talk to Julie and her boyfriends about reproduction, so long as their parents knew what I'm doing. I think it would be a good idea for you to be there as well. Those boys will listen to a man if they won't me."

"Carolyn, darling?"

"Yes?"

"All this talk about ... you know ... is having an effect on me."

She hesitated before realizing what a randy husband she had.

"Oh, yes, I see," Carolyn said, blushing.

She quickly gathered herself.

"I was trying to have a serious discussion about our children, and you decide to get cute. Sometimes I wonder what kind of man I married! Are you or are you not going to talk to the boys?"

He smiled at her. The kind of sheepish grin she'd seen many times before. A smile that suggested he took her point, but he still wanted to be cute.

'Very boyish,' she thought. A big part of the reason she loved him.

He shrugged in a suggestive way, and they both laughed. It slightly embarrassed Carolyn to know what would likely follow.

§

About those proposed talks with Julie's male and female friends? Well, they never happened. Not ever. Carolyn had finally stopped digging and put away her shovel.

PART V
TRIALS

24 DISCORDANCE

Like termites that slowly gnaw away the wooden foundation of a home, something short of outright incompatibility had lurked just below the surface of Carolyn and Conrad's marriage from the beginning. Call the source of discordance social or cultural, for it was both, but mostly the peril came from the constraints of history that neither partner could fully grasp or alter. Call it destiny ... karma.

Sam Profit had glimpsed it, some of it at least, and managed to hold his tongue—for the most part. The job of controlling Sam's impetuosity fell to Abigail Profit. Both of Carolyn's parents sensed the danger and sought to protect their daughter in their own way.

Then, Sam and Abigail were gone, and Carolyn believed she had to maintain her independence as a Profit and leverage the cultural superiority—elitism—she felt as a Daughter of the American Revolution.

Now, however, hanging ominously over everything in this improbable union was the war just ended. She never spoke openly of it, of course, but in Carolyn's unconscious mind her husband's 'people' had unleashed a catastrophe on most of the world. Her husband was not merely an immigrant and coal man, but a 'son' of the German Kaiser.

At the heart of the couple's discordance lay Carolyn's desire to keep Conrad's family at arm's length for her own comfort, it seemed, and for the sake of her children. Carolyn viewed the Bauers, excepting her husband, as little short of social and cultural misbegotten. Georg and his oldest son, Pieter, were shoemakers; skilled, yes, but uneducated. The extended Bauer family and the Profits had nothing in common. They had never been close except for the union of Carolyn and Conrad.

Carolyn's reservations about her husband's background did not in any way diminish her love for Conrad Bauer. She had loved him from the moment he caught her frolicking at the water trough—even before. Conrad was ambitious, capable, and a good provider. And in youth, dashing and fun! But the Bauers were shoemakers and coal men, peasants at root, a fact about the family that would never change in her unconscious mind.

What gave each of them an absolutist sense of superiority? Just who was Carolyn to be so snooty? Many things, of course. But when she thought of the Bauers, she also thought of herself as the opposite, a DAR, another fact not subject to change. When her parents died, Carolyn told Conrad she'd never return to Griggs. He thought her ultimatum peculiar since his family lived there, a family to which she belonged, and one he had no intention of abandoning.

Every three or four months, Carolyn and Conrad had 'the conversation' about visiting Conrad's family in Griggs. Every three or four months, the result was the same.

"Another letter from Mother, Carolyn. She'd like us to come up when we can. How about it? Will you come with me this time? Mother says she'd very much like to see you and the children."

"Oh, Conrad," she sighed. "It's always the same. I don't know your family well enough," she rationalized. "It's my fault, I know, but I'm just not comfortable with them in their house."

"Isn't that the point of your going? To get to know them better?"

"I know them, but we have nothing in common."

"Aren't you and I something in common?"

Carolyn began to cry. He recognized it as her way of ending 'the conversation.'

He knew what had gone unsaid. Carolyn just didn't think the Bauers were good enough for her or her children. He didn't like it. He resented it. It confirmed the void in their marriage that he suspected. 'We have nothing in common.' The echo of her words shattered him. The Bauers, none of them, were good enough for Carolyn and *his* children? The implication was obvious, but he said nothing ... each time.

So, Conrad Bauer packed his carpet bag of a predominately red, paisley design and took the train to Griggs—again and alone.

§

When she considered the Bauers of Griggs, Carolyn sculpted her view of Conrad's family in the clay of irrationality. She tried to keep her bias private, but there were those occasional leaks, such as discussions of their going to Griggs together.

It seemed not to have occurred to Carolyn that her family, too, had descended from immigrants long before anyone heard of the DAR. Nor did it occur that Georg and Pieter Bauer were as skilled at their trade as Sam Profit was his. And hadn't her husband shown skill in putting together a career in coal that positioned him to run a successful business in Sioux City?

And what of Conrad? Had he reason to think badly of the DAR, its members, and their laudable works? In truth, neither camp, Bauer and Profit, had any historical basis on which they could rest claims of superiority, although Carolyn's bias had always been clearer.

§

Who were the 'Bauers' before they came to live in Bierstadt, Baden-Württemberg in southwest Germany? Did they ... Did Conrad have reason to feel superior to the DAR?

The Chicago *Tribune*, September 20, 1919—

In what the Romans called Germania, the inhabitants had built wooden houses, farmed, and used no written language or money (peasants all).

Then, the 5th century ushered in the *Völkerwanderung* ('migration of peoples') throughout Europe. The Huns, who no one ever accused of being noble, swept across eastern Europe; German-speaking tribes began pressing west into the Roman provinces.

Over the next four centuries, a string of Frankish (Germanic-speaking) kings, including Charlemagne, expanded their holdings in Western Europe, bringing Christianity in their wake (peasants beware).

Eventually, 'Louis the German,' received the eastern part of his grandfather Charlemagne's claims; his became the medieval Kingdom of Germany, the largest piece of the Holy Roman Empire.

Although the Black Death killed a third or more of the region's population in the mid-14th century (mostly peasants), the population of Germany had doubled by the 16th century. Then, more division and killing (of peasants).

Following the Protestant Reformation, the mid-16th century Peace of Augsburg tried to end the violent religious conflicts by allowing each state's ruler to decide its religion. Still, a regional 'rebellion' over religion ('Thirty Years War') escaped its assigned boundaries and ravaged Germany. A 'regional rebellion' left up to a third of Germany's population (peasants) dead from war, sickness, or starvation, and unleashed waves of emigration.

> Not until 1871 did the German states coalesce into one imperial state, leading to truly catastrophic years of hubris for which millions of ordinary Germans, British Tommies, French Poilus (peasants all), and many, many others paid a hefty price: *Deutschland Über Alles* → 1914-18.

§

And where exactly lay the nobility of Carolyn and Ezra Allen's ancestors? Did they have sufficient of blood that allowed them to look down on the Bauers? The answer was an eerie echo.

> The Chicago *Tribune*, September 21, 1919—
> Start with the Romans. What peoples did they find when they invaded the British Isles? Nobility? Of course not. They routed the remnants of hunter-gatherer and tribal societies: peasants—pathetically weak ones.
> When the Romans withdrew from Britannia in the 5th century, presumably after installing a 'nobility,' tribes from ... Yes! Tribes from northern Germany stepped into the void. The Germanic Angles and Saxons soon controlled much of the former Roman territory and imposed their language and customs on the local inhabitants much as the Romans had. Powerful Germans had again conquered English peasants. But those Anglo-Saxons didn't last long, either.
> By the early 11th century, the Vikings who had settled in northern France (called Danelaw), and were more familiarly known as Normans, ruled their piece of France with the sanction of the French crown. Neither had any use for

> Anglo-Saxon kings. Thus, the end of the English Germans drew nigh.
>
> That end came—except for the brief but legendary resistance of Robin Hood (a noble) and his Merry Band (peasants) who prevented it for a time—when the ambitious Normans, led by William the Conqueror, crossed the English Channel, defeated Harold Godwinson at the Battle of Hastings in 1066 (many dead peasants) and claimed the throne of England.
>
> The Norman kings, ruling primarily from France, eventually gave rise to the House of Plantagenet, which continued in power until the end of the 15th century, when Henry Tudor defeated Richard III at the Battle of Bosworth Field (more dead peasants), took the throne as Henry VII, and ushered in the reign of the House of Tudor (executions of nobility for a change, in the form of uncooperative queens). That lasted until 1603.
>
> While Tudor-Stuart kings and a queen (Elizabeth I) wrestled over religious faith and a crown, England became a major naval power with its defeat of the 'invincible' Spanish Armada in 1588 by Lord Charles Howard and Sir Francis Drake. That action positioned the island to compete for territories of its own. The next three and a half centuries of hubris cost millions of ordinary Englishmen and colonials (peasants all) a hefty price in lives lost: English superiority and dominion (India and Africa in particular) → 'Rule Britannia'→ the 'Great War.'

Thus, two cultures—truly one if looked at in the broadest sense—nearly committed suicide in pursuit of 'noble' causes. Should Carolyn and the DAR have turned their noses up at the peasantry of Europe (what remained of it) and its transplants in the American Midwest in obeisance to such dubious nobility? Wasn't it possible that Ezra Allen of Valley Forge was a peasant in the same vein as Georg, Pieter, and Konrad Bauer? If so—and it does seem likely—what gave Carolyn, by way of the DAR, the right to disdain the Bauers of Griggs and, by inference, her husband? That was a question Conrad had to ask himself repeatedly, for he dared not ask it of his wife, a question on which his marriage teetered ... Discordance ... Improbability ...

25 THE 'DAUGHTERS'

Despite its discordant role in the Bauer marriage, Carolyn, both unaware of and disinterested in the history of 'nobility' just told, brushed aside as much friction as she dared. She believed instinctively, like a bird teaching its chicks to fly, that the time had come to educate her daughter about the Daughters of the American Revolution or DAR (Conrad be damned). Eventually, Julie would have to decide how she felt about joining.

"By now, Julie," Carolyn's instruction began, "you've learned in school about the American Revolution and its principles. For those of us whose roots connect to that conflict, the DAR preserves and promotes those ideals. I belong. Whether you will want to join is strictly up to you. I do have to warn you that your father takes a dim view of it."

"What does he say? What are his objections? It seems like a worthy organization."

"I'll only say he believes the DAR is exclusive, snobby and elitist. I've explained to him that the main purposes are historic preservation, education and patriotism. But, you know, your father came from Germany at a very young age, so he has no ties to American history. That makes it hard for him to understand those of us who do have those ties."

"He's never talked about that with me, Mother. How old was he when he came?"

"Eleven. What do you remember about your life before you were eleven?"

"Not much, really. Some parties. Fun in the snow."

"Father's family in Germany was very poor. My family was not. His father was a shoemaker in a small village, and when he died, the family decided they needed to leave, believing America would offer them an opportunity to get back on their feet, so to speak."

"Uncle Peter is a shoemaker, right?"

"Yes, he came over first, established himself in Griggs as the only shoemaker in town. Then, Grandma Bauer, Marta, Louise, and your father came a couple of years later. Those last two years in Bierstadt were tough, as they had only some savings to get by on."

"That helps me to understand his objections to the DAR. Thank you for telling me."

"Of course. And, as you know by now, because you are hearing it from me and not him, your father never speaks of those things. I believe it's not because he doesn't remember them, so much as it is he wants really to be an American. Just not the DAR version of America. I'd say he's very much an egalitarian."

Julie let that sink in. She realized that her egalitarian intuitions had something to do with her father.

"If I decide to join the DAR, what are the requirements?"

"There are strict rules: Only direct female descendants—they call it proof of lineal descent—of Revolutionary soldiers or participants in Revolutionary causes are eligible for membership. The DAR defines 'patriot'—participant—as anyone who helped to achieve America's independence. But you know all that."

"You must also be 18 before gaining approval from your chapter; that is, the chapter in which you seek membership. They vote you in or out, but if out, you can reapply to any of the other DAR chapters—there are hundreds."

"I wonder why they would vote you out."

"Maybe they discovered something about your character that didn't suit them. Maybe you've been in trouble with the police. Probably it would have something to do with your proof, your application ... things like that."

"When did it start and why?"

"I think in 1890. As I understand it, after the wounds of the Civil War had begun to heal, patriotism burst back in full force when the Civil War had been over for a while. The country began to feel more nationalistic, which rested in great part on a desire to understand the beginnings of the country's independence ...

"Now, here's where the DAR came in. Aggravated at their exclusion from male-only ancestry—patriotic—organizations, many women decided to form their own. It wasn't only Revolutionary men they chose to honor, but women patriots as well ...

"The last thing I wanted to stress before you must finish your homework and I must get supper on the table are the organization's goals. I'd say there are three: education with an emphasis on youth, instilling patriotism, and historical preservation—cultural heritage. Okay?"

"Do you think the DAR looks down on people who do not have a Revolutionary participant? Is Father correct? Are they snooty?"

"I certainly don't think so, but he does, to a degree. And to whatever extent that may be, I haven't been able to convince him otherwise."

Not intending to suggest Julie choose sides, Carolyn wisely decided not to involve her further in her parent's disagreement over this issue. There were far more important aspects of their relationship—romance, for example—to which a young woman like Julie, beginning puberty, should pay attention.

§

"Father?" Julie said one morning at breakfast when her mother had gone upstairs to gather clothes for washing and the boys still slept. It was a rare private moment.

"Yes, Honey?"

"Do you remember coming over from Germany when you were a child?"

"Why do you ask me that?" he said irritably. "Have you been talking to Grandma or Aunt Louise? I don't suppose Uncle Peter. He wasn't with us."

"No, none of them. I just wondered, that's all. Do you remember anything about it?"

"You know, Honey, this is quite remarkable. In all these years since, including those I have known your mother, *no* one ... and I mean NO one ever asked me that question."

She didn't say so, of course, but Julie found what he'd just said astonishing. She saw how the neglect of such a moment in his life pained her father deeply.

"Really?" she said, the sadness in her voice obvious.

Conrad knew he must answer her. He wanted to answer her. He put down his napkin and fork, and leaned back in his chair, never taking his eye off his daughter. Julie could almost see the wheels of memory spinning in his head. He seemed a million miles away.

"This may surprise you, Julie. I was a small boy, but I wasn't blind or dumb. I remember *everything* about that trip," he began softly. "I ... Sorry. I meant to say *we* have a good life in Sioux City. We have plenty of food, a solid roof over our heads, you have a beautiful school to attend, as do the boys. Mother has her friends who also have all those things. I have a job that supports us ...

"Now, and this is the important part, I want you to imagine our lives as if *none* of that were true. *None!* Tuck away *everything* we have. It doesn't exist."

As he said to 'tuck away everything,' he spread his arms wide, nearly toppling over in his chair, then righted himself.

"Can you do that. I expect it will be hard."

"I think I can, Father."

"Good. I want you to keep thinking about it."

"Yes, Father."

"Are you trying hard to tuck away everything we have somewhere, a place from which it cannot be retrieved ... ever?"

"I hope so. I'm trying."

"Alright, when you have done that, you will know what I remember about that voyage. Do you understand what I'm saying?"

"You're telling me you remember unimaginable poverty. You're telling me you had nothing. But I also think none of you were poor in courage or ambition, but you haven't said that."

"Apparently, I have a clever daughter, and I didn't need to say those words. Julie, Honey, everyone in this country should have been on a voyage such as that one. Yes, I was a miserable wretch, a fact I readily acknowledge, and I behaved wretchedly, truths that Grandma will confirm. But there were hundreds of others on that ship in far worse circumstances than me. I might have died had it not been for Grandma, but dozens of others who did not have someone like your grandmother did perish. Such were their lives it probably came to them as a blessing."

"Is that trip why you think so little of the DAR?"

"Ah, ha! I see you *have* been talking to your mother. Let's put it this way and then drop it. No one from the DAR was on that voyage. No one from the DAR was ever in Bierstadt. They have their heritage, to be sure, and

I respect that. But they will never truly know people like me."

"Doesn't Mother know you?"

"Have you asked her that?"

"No, not in so many words."

"Julie, we love each other, your mother and me. That's all I need, and I think she feels the same. I don't talk about the DAR, but I have my opinion of it. And, as I told you earlier, I don't talk about that voyage. Let's leave it there, okay?"

Julie paused before speaking again.

"Father, have you ever read *Silas Marner*? It's a short story by George Eliot."

"No, why?"

"Oh, no reason. Just wondering. I think you might like it."

26   SAY, 'AHH'

Marta Bauer Clark awoke to a rainy, late September morning. Outside, an occasional zephyr below her bedroom window picked up the wet leaves and put them where they didn't belong. An omen, perhaps? Her husband Ray had already left for work at Jacobs, the only clothing store in Griggs.

    Their oldest son, Philip, who had taken breakfast with his father, headed off for school, kicking those wet leaves—elms, maples, and sycamores—off the sidewalk. A fruitless endeavor, he discovered. When he returned home, his mother would have something to say about the damage to his shoes.

Billy, Marta and Ray's youngest, lingered in bed. That was unusual for a boy of ten who needed to get his breakfast down and join his brother at school.

When Marta entered the boy's bedroom, Billy told her in a weak voice that he didn't feel well.

"Where do you feel bad, Honey. Is it a tummy ache?"

"Sort of, but my throat is sore, and I've been coughing. Sometimes I get cold and shake. And my head hurts."

She placed her palm across his forehead.

"I think I'd better take your temperature."

She went to the bathroom. She found the thermometer in the closet, just where it should have been, and after the required amount of time under Billy's tongue, she removed it and shuddered. It read 102°.

"I'm going to call Doctor Miller's office. I'll be right back. Do you want some tea before I go? A piece of toast? Those might make you feel a little better."

"Yes," he said softly, which started a cough. He swallowed. "Please."

Marta fixed the tea and buttered his toast, made sure Billy was drinking and eating, then picked up the telephone to consult with Doctor Miller.

§

In the spring of 1918, months before Billy Clark complained of a sore throat and chills, doctors in Madrid, Spain began to note a particularly virulent influenza spreading among the country's population.

§

William Miller, a native of Sparta, Wisconsin, had been practicing in Griggs since graduating from the University of Minnesota Medical School. Normally, he tried to see patients in their homes as well as his office, and he made no exception in the case of Billy Clark.

Miller, a tall, gentle man who wore wire-rimmed glasses, had delivered into that world most of the kids in town of Billy's age. He was best known among his 'progeny' for the magical black bag he carried on every house call. Once at his destination, and with an impish smile, he'd deliberately and slowly open that bag. Inside it resembled a sophisticated fisherman's tackle box.

The practiced choreography, the sly prestidigitation involved in the careful unsealing of that bag next to Doc Miller's leg, could be seen as having two purposes: a sneaky way to get kids to forget how bad they felt; or a 'cure' for the slackers or the psychosomatic—those who just didn't want to go to school.

A suspicion existed among some townspeople that Doc Miller, conjurer extraordinaire, *wanted* to mystify his patients, especially the smaller ones, with that black bag. *Hocus-pocus* you're cured. For many parents, that was the promise of Doc Miller's bag.

At Billy's bedside, Doc Miller bent to the task, and gradually, multiple trays of small boxes and corked bottles revealed themselves, seated in offset, layered trays on either side. The further he opened the bag, the more boxes and bottles that showed themselves. Every kid that Philip and Billy knew could describe this event in detail, sometimes in gory detail because of the different colors of the elixirs inside and the imaginations of children. None were hesitant to proffer uneducated guesses as to what those corked bottles contained.

Miller began his examination of Billy with a wooden tongue depressor, 'Say, ahh,' and a stethoscope he had already pulled from the bag. With every move carefully checked by the wide-eyed kid at hand, he deftly hung the two metal prongs around either side of his neck, attaching one side and then the other—all with one hand! Incredible!

"Say, ahh again, Billy," Miller gently ordered.

He swabbed Billy's cheek with the cottony end of a stick.

"Ahh … Ouch! That hurts!"

"The swab or your throat?"

"Both," and he began to cry.

Miller dropped the swab into a bottle containing one of those mysterious liquids, then he listened to Billy's back and chest. He told Marta he needed some sputum that we need the lab to check.

"Have Billy cough and spit into this bottle. Bring it to the office as soon as you can."

Miller closed his bag with a resounding snap, and he and Marta left the room.

"Has he described any other symptoms?"

"Yes, quite surprisingly in some detail: headache, chills, sore throat, and a cough.

"Well, yes, I can confirm the sore throat. It's quite red. I'm certain it's a mild case of the flu, but as there have been reports of something more serious, checking his sputum is crucial. Do you understand?"

"Yes, of course, doctor."

Marta did as Miller asked. Then she called Ray at the factory and her mother.

By 7:40 that evening Billy Clark's lungs had filled with liquid, and Marta wasn't feeling well.

Billy died of acute viral pneumonia at 9:01 P.M. Gone! In one day! Marta collapsed from emotional exhaustion and a temperature of 103°. Anna Maria, who had also been at Billy's side since Doctor Miller's house call, stayed with Philip while Ray rushed Marta to the hospital in Bismarck.

It was too late. The next morning Anna Maria telegraphed Conrad the terrible news. His sister and his nephew were gone. In one day! He packed his carpetbag again, his mind in a daze. Another lonely trip, although this time with a double tragedy on his mind, not Carolyn's refusal to relate to his family, even in this awful circumstance. *That* he kept in the back of his mind. Something between him and Carolyn came near to breaking that day, something that neither could fix. He wept all the way to Griggs.

§

The people of Griggs and hundreds of towns across North Dakota had some warning of what lay ahead that fall. They waited in what amounted to a catatonic state for signs of the deadly contagion that had been circulating in the country since March. Their anxiety overshadowed the autumn ritual of watching leaves turn color as the weather became sharp.

On Sept. 27, the day Billy Clark passed away, Minnesota reported its first influenza case, a single soldier home on leave. Train travel and transoceanic ships carrying hundreds of thousands of troops enabled much of the rapid spread. Then, cases began appearing throughout the state. Soon, many in Minnesota and North Dakota would share Carolyn's lament: "It's this damned war."

Townspeople in Griggs knew their time had come when, in addition to Billy Clark, Dr. William Miller announced 20 more cases. By Oct. 5, newspapers reported that North Dakota confronted thousands of cases.

Most of those who fell ill recovered. But those like Billy Clark often died in a few hours. As the uncontrolled infection spread, panic settled in. Deaths only mounted, and panic turned into desperation.

§

> The Bismarck *Tribune*, October 7, 1918—
> The Spanish flu was at least than twenty times more likely to cause death than other influenzas. It caused a terrible form of pneumonia that suffocated patients. Within a year, the Spanish flu became a world-wide pandemic that killed between 20 and 40 million people. The death rate in North Dakota was lower than in some large cities, but it was nevertheless as devastating as in other parts of the world.
> Troop movements fostered the spread of the disease, and the war had laid waste sanitation, health systems, and devoured doctors and nurses. In Minnesota and North Dakota, a third of the doctors and nurses who were supporting the war effort, leaving communities with a severe shortage of health professionals. Few small towns had hospitals, or more than one doctor. Private duty nurses assigned to care for patients

in their own homes by physicians or the Red Cross supplied the standard method of patient care. Neighbors of the sick and schoolteachers filled in to relieve exhausted physicians. Teachers volunteering as nurses set up emergency hospitals.

Health officials recommended that people rest, use handkerchiefs, go to bed when ill, and call their doctors if symptoms worsened. As the pandemic spread, people were advised not to gather in crowds, spit on floors or sidewalks or share drinking cups or towels. In Minnesota, three funerals stemming from one wedding illustrated the hazards of social gatherings, which the appropriate authorities hadn't banned in time to avoid such tragedies.

§

One night, when Doc Miller believed the worst in his town and state had passed, he switched on a small light on the stand next to his bed. It was 2:45 A.M.

"What's happening?" his wife Jean asked, sleepily.

"I'll just be a minute."

Miller took out his diary from a drawer in the stand. He paused to think for a moment, and then jotted down a cryptic entry: 'North Dakota, 1,378 official deaths, possibly 5,000.'

PART VI
SIBLINGS

27   JULIE

The deaths of Abigail and Samuel, the war, and the Spanish flu dealt a series of severe blows to the Bauers and Clarks of Griggs. They had come to know that legendary horseman—death—astride its pale horse. In Sioux City, the string of catastrophes, personal and universal, only widened the rift between Carolyn and Conrad.

Anna Maria, Peter, Louise, and Conrad laid Marta and Billy to rest. Carolyn didn't attend the joint funeral, but she sent two sprays of flowers and notes, the first addressed to Anna Maria. It included a surprising *mea culpa*, which had the disappointing effect of not repairing her strained relationship with Conrad's mother:

Dear Mother Bauer,

I don't have the words necessary to express the profound sorrow I feel at the loss of your daughter and grandson. I can offer, I believe, a silver lining to the dark cloud of your grief. Perhaps you will find in it some consolation and a hopeful way of looking at the future.

Marta and Billy are gone, yes, but a person much wiser than me once said that not long from now, when you think of those who have left us, the memory of them will turn your tears into a smile. I hope you will find joy in the lives of your remaining family.

I realize that what I want to say next you may think inappropriate in a letter of condolence. But it is something that I believe I need to say, and it does come from the same place—my heart—as the words I spoke on your terrible loss.

I have not been a worthy daughter-in-law, one that you richly deserve, a confession which will come as no surprise to you. For that, I have great shame and no excuse other than an overrated sense of myself. It may be too late in my life to change or to make right my past snubs, but I shall try very hard.

I especially wish you to know that on this sad occasion, I am sending you flowers that represent a warm embrace. May your tears soon become that smile.

Affectionately, Carolyn

Carolyn penned a similar note to Ray Clark, worded to address his loss.

Anna Maria considered the sincerity of Carolyn's words, but she remained skeptical. If Carolyn wanted to mend her ways, wouldn't the funerals have supplied an obvious opportunity?

My Dear Carolyn,

Thank you for your kind words of sympathy. They meant much to me and the Griggs family, with whom I shared your note. I hope you don't mind that I did so.

As for your 'overrated sense of self,' we here in Griggs look forward to seeing you, too, when Conrad next makes the journey.

Your flowers and the message they carried were, in turn, lovely and warmly received. Thank you.

Sincerely, Anna Maria Bauer

§

The Bauers of Sioux City were not a wealthy family, but Conrad's business, Bauer Coal, had met with enough success to support a comfortable, middle-class life. Although Conrad's was not the only coal distributor in Sioux City, his fleet of six trucks, all bearing the stenciled family name on either front door, commanded a sufficient share of business in the city.

Conrad had one regret about the business after the family moved to Iowa. Neither John Charles, 16 in 1919, nor Peter Samuel, 14 the same year, had shown the slightest interest in coal. And Julie? Well, she made no secret of her regard for her father's business (it's dirty!), a prejudice that began, Conrad was convinced, with her Profit grandparents.

Julie's life was undergoing enormous change. From the sidelines she cheered and supported her mother's suffragist activity. It was her fervent hope that as she was about to turn twenty-one, she would be able to vote. Conrad had mixed feelings about his radical wife and daughter. He supported suffrage for women, but he wasn't thrilled with the attention his wife's activities had on his business. Sioux City was no bastion of suffragist sentiment.

§

Julie had cut her political teeth from the sidelines of suffragist marches and protests. But it wasn't North Dakota that led the way for women. Wyoming shared that honor with Montana.

The Cowboy State, the first to allow women the right to vote, entered the Union in 1890 with its suffrage laws intact. And 1n 1916 the Mountain State elected Janette Rankin as the first woman to serve in Congress.

Still, women continued to go to jail for their activism, and the House passed a suffrage amendment in January 1918 amid World War I by a healthy margin, 274 to 136, which the Senate rejected. Rankin chastised her colleagues:

> *"How shall we answer [the Senate's] challenge, gentlemen: how shall we explain to them the meaning of democracy if the same Congress that voted for war to make the world safe for democracy refuses to give this small measure of democracy to the women of our country?"*

But Julie and women like her persevered, and the measure, reintroduced in the House, passed on May 21, 1919, by a vote of 304 to 90. The Senate concurred shortly afterward. The 19th Amendment then went to the states. On August 26, 1920, as Julie awaited her sophomore year at Kansas, Tennessee became the thirty-sixth state to ratify the 19th Amendment. Women across the country could vote!

"Just don't expect me to vote like you!" Carolyn voiced her personal declaration of political independence to her husband. The poor man got the second of a double-barrel blast. "And when Julie is old enough, don't expect *her* to follow your lead. That was the whole point of the 19th. Independence! Manumission!"

§

While the drama of female suffrage played out, Julie had begun to stake out a new life for herself at college, the first female among the Profits and Bauers to do so. At age eighteen in 1919, she had moved to Lawrence to enroll in the University of Kansas.

Julie planned to continue her earlier interest in Margaret Sanger. She wanted to know more about Sanger's ideas related to birth control, but beyond that she wanted to know how Sanger connected that issue to the role of women in society more broadly. The latter brought Janette Rankin into Julie's consciousness. Sanger and Rankin became Julie's heroes. Not Wilson, not Taft, and certainly not Warren Harding when he oozed into the political world.

Why the University of Kansas? Prior to enrolling she had perused a variety of course catalogues, page by page, looking for classes, or just *a* class, devoted to women's issues. Julie didn't find anything that she could interpret as 'women's studies,' but she did discover at nearby Kansas the discipline that might eventually get her there: sociology. That seemed the obvious course of study.

So, Julie's choice of Kansas was no accident. The oldest continuing sociology course in the United States began at Kansas in 1890, and the faculty inaugurated a Department of History and Sociology the following year. But Kansas was following a movement whose origin lay elsewhere.

A course entitled 'sociology' had been taught for the first time in the United States in 1875 by William Graham Sumner, and the first full-fledged independent university department of sociology was established in 1892 at the University of Chicago.

A Most Improbable Union 189

The University of Chicago encouraged sociologists to study the society around them. Chicago directed their attention to the individual and promoted equal rights. The program combined with other departments to offer students well-rounded studies requiring courses in hegemony, economics, psychology, multiple social sciences, and political science.

When Julie read that, she shrieked with delight. Her eye caught it at once. Hegemony! That sounded to her like the hegemony of the patriarchy. Wasn't that part of Sanger's concern?

Then, a wholly unexpected thing happened, an intellectual U-turn, a deflection from Sanger to a Negro sociologist named W.E.B. DuBois. Julie's 'discovery' of the Negro struck her like a bolt of lightning.

> *The New York Times*, April 23, 1905—
> W.E.B. DuBois's *The Philadelphia Negro* (1899), was the first scientific study of African Americans and a major contribution to early scientific sociology in the United States. In it, DuBois coined the phrase 'the submerged tenth' to describe the Negro underclass. Later, in 1903,

> DuBois popularized the term, the 'Talented Tenth,' by which he meant society's elite class. DuBois's terminology reflected his opinion that the elites of a nation, both Negro and white, were critical to achievements in culture and progress.
>
> Then, to underscore in bold, black type his point about the genius and humanity of the Negro race, DuBois published *The Souls of Black Folk* (1903), which set forth two core ideas: that 'the problem of the Twentieth Century was the problem of the color line'; and the dual consciousness lived by Negroes—American and Negro. DuBois argued this duality was unique, a handicap in the past, yes, but a strength in the future.

DuBois's work startled the unworldly young woman from Griggs, North Dakota, by way of Sioux City, Iowa. Julie struggled to understand whether DuBois had unlocked a great truth, or truths. If so, what did it portend?

Sanger, Rankin, DuBois, a trifecta of earth-shattering challengers to the young, and until then unworldly mind of Julie Bauer. That she was both star-struck and overwhelmed at the tender age of eighteen would only begin to describe what had happened to Julie as the 'war to end all war' and the Spanish flu, which had not been kind to her family, slipped into 'a return to normalcy.' There would be nothing normal about Julie's life after Kansas.

28 JOHN & PETER

Carolyn and Conrad's home had begun to resemble an empty nest by 1921. John left for college, but he did not follow his sister to Kansas. Instead, he chose the University of Illinois, as did Peter two years later. Nor would their educations bring them close to having an interest in visionary thinkers and activists like Margaret Sanger and W.E.B. DuBois who had moved their sister. Rather, John and Peter chose the business curriculum. They hadn't been interested in their father's coal business, but they did envision opportunities of a 'cleaner' sort after graduation.

The war had ended before it could take their lives, as, sadly, it had millions of others their age. During their college years, however, both young men faced a problem directly related to the war that Julie had not: name prejudice. Bauer! There was a kind of juvenile cruelty about many aspects of fraternity life during and after the bloody war. One of the worst and most prevalent was name shaming.

§

The New York Times, June 21, 1923—
The Commerce Department, which conducted each decennial census, estimated in 1910 that one in every eleven Americans was first or second-generation German; Germans were the largest, non-English speaking immigrant group in America. Several Midwest cities had German-language schools. German-language newspapers, and even clubs where German Americans could enjoy their own company while drinking German-style lager thrived in those same cities. German Catholic and Lutheran churches often operated as schools, teaching their German-American students in German.

Despite all this, in the years leading up to and during World War I, the United States experienced a wave of anti-German sentiment, fueled by super patriotism and xenophobia that

> resulted in open hostility toward all things German.
>
> Americans no longer felt that German culture could mix with American society. Anglo-Americans began to fear that German Americans were still loyal to the *Kaiser*, the German emperor. These sentiments became even stronger after the United States joined the war on the side of the Allies against Germany, the most powerful of the Central Powers. German Americans became a perceived security threat. They bore taunts, various forms of violence, threats of death, and death itself. And they got a new nickname: 'the Hun.'

For John and Peter, the taunts and violence never reached the most extreme level, as it did for so many other German Americans. But they believed the cruel mocking of their name, the slight change in its spelling, might present a roadblock to business careers.

"Father," Peter asked, "did you ever have people doubt your loyalty because of your name?"

"They call us all sorts of other names: 'Krauts, Heinies, Huns. Those are just a few," John chimed in.

Carolyn listened from the kitchen where she was plucking feathers for tomorrow's traditional fried chicken dinner. Thus far, Conrad was silent.

"What's that fraternity you joined?" she asked.

"Lambda Delta Mu," John replied.

"And what is the definition of 'fraternity'?" Conrad asked, finally, from his chair in the living room.

Both brothers hesitated.

"Brotherhood, you dopes!" he yelled impatiently. "Look up the word 'fraternal.'"

Both had dictionaries in the bedroom they shared. John was the first to answer his father.

"A 'fraternal organization' is, quoting from Webster's, 'an organized society of men associated together in an environment of companionship and brotherhood.' There's more, but that seems the main point."

"Exactly," Conrad said. "Now, does what you've been experiencing in the way of name calling seem 'fraternal' to you? And if not, I suggest you find some other 'brothers' and another place to live."

"But it's not just the Lambdas, Father. We get it everywhere on campus," Peter replied. "Even some professors."

"I have another suggestion," Carolyn interjected.

With that, she was about to say something that would only add fuel to the smoldering embers of the class differences she had always believed existed between her and Conrad.

Conrad rose and walked to the kitchen.

"I know where you're going with this, Carolyn, but don't. They must learn to cope on their own. When they get out there in the business world, no one is going to throw them a rope to keep them from drowning. They'll have to be strong, independent, and if you're going to say what I think you're going to say, please don't, for their sakes, not mine."

§

Six months later Carolyn took her sons to the Woodbury County Courthouse on Douglas Street. The clerk, a Mr. Pool ... Clarence Pool, had scheduled a date for their appearance before the judge.

Prior to their appointment, John and Peter had filled out change of name forms, which required them to write down a cause.

What they wrote both did and did not reveal the rift in the Bauer family. They wrote 'teasing' and 'harassment,' but those were not what lay behind Carolyn's push for the change. From the beginning of their lives, her demeanor had instilled in her children the notion they were of a class apart from others, especially those less well-educated, those who drew a paycheck rather than commanding a salary, and those with foreign-sounding names. They would never forget those subtle principles.

The Bauer brothers filed the forms with the court clerk along with a fee. Everything was pro forma. A judge had reviewed their forms and agreed to the change prior to their appearance.

Clarence Pool met them in the hallway and invited them into his office. Pool met every stereotypical quality alleged of a clerk: short, no jacket, white shirt, its sleeve lengths controlled by elastic garters, watch chain hung across a striped waistcoat, clashing trousers, unshined black shoes.

"Excuse me, Ma'am, you're the young men's mother, am I correct?" Pool asked as he looked over the applications.

"Yes, Mrs. Bauer."

"Oh, I see, more Germans changing their name."

"I don't see how that's any of your business, Mister ...? Does the judge know you talk to people like that?"

"I apologize, Ma'am. It won't happen again."

Abigail Profit's memory flashed before Carolyn.

"And don't 'Ma'am' me! I'm *not* a Madam!"

"No, Ma' ..." He stopped short and flushed, realizing he was digging the hole he had already started even deeper. "No, Mrs. Bauer. I apologize."

The clerk couldn't wait to end his conversation with Carolyn.

"Okay," the clerk continued, as he turned to the boys, "the judge has approved your petitions. Be sure to put your new name on all personal and legal documents, and notify your school ... You are in school, right?"

"Yes, sir."

"Yes, sir."

"No need to call me 'sir.' The only one who gets that honor in this building is His Honor, Judge Elwood Thomas ...

"Now, you should also notify the Post Office, and any bank where you have an account, the tax collector—very important—the Registrar of Voters, and the Passport Office if you plan on leaving the country."

John and Peter's hearing before Judge Thomas ended quickly. Thomas asked only a few questions. Most importantly, he wanted an assurance the petition was truthful, and the young men were not changing to defraud anyone.

Assurances given, John, Peter, and Carolyn returned to the clerk's office, a small room off the courtroom and Thomas's chambers.

"Now," the clerk continued, "you need to file the judge's signed order granting the change and provide copies for every institution or person needing proof of that change. Keep a certified copy for your personal files and record the change order with the Woodbury County Auditor. That's it. You are officially Mr. John Charles Bower, and Mr. Peter Samuel Bower. Congratulations!"

The clerk shook their hand and grinned sheepishly at Carolyn.

"Come on, boys, let's get out of here before he tries to call me 'Ma'am' again!"

§

"So, 'Bauer' not good enough for you, huh?" Conrad greeted Carolyn and his sons at the front door when they returned from the courthouse.

"Let me talk to your father alone. And don't worry …"

"Conrad, please, don't do this. Of course, your name is 'good enough' for me, as you put it. But this was not about you or me. It's about our sons who went through a lot of torment at college. They genuinely believe the only way they can put that behind them and have secure futures is to make the change …

"It's just a slight change in spelling, Conrad, and it sounds the same. Your sons love you! They would never do anything to slight your background and everything you've accomplished, of which they are very proud, as I am."

"Honey?"

Conrad squeezed Carolyn's hand.

"Yes?"

"You think I should do it, too, don't you?"

She didn't see that one coming.

"Not on your life, Conrad Bauer! You'd have to re-stencil all your trucks!"

Conrad threw his head back in laughter.

§

Carolyn had good reason to think seriously about ending the toxic atmosphere poisoning her marriage. She was about to learn the tension with Conrad had *not* escaped the attention of their children They did not share their mother's superior attitude or their father's criticism of the DAR. Peter Samuel raised the issue with his mother.

"Mother," he began tremulously, "you do realize that Julie, John, and I worry about the obvious tension between you and Father."

Carolyn turned slowly toward her youngest son. She wasn't sure she'd heard him correctly.

"Did you hear me, Mother?"

"Yes, of course."

That was only half true. She heard the words but not their meaning.

"We know you must still love each other very much, but we see the looks, and we hear your tone and Father's sarcasm. It hurts."

Carolyn's eyes grew misty; she realized how selfish they'd been. She and Conrad had never considered how their children viewed their marriage.

"Peter, I'm so sorry! We never thought about the three of you. I suppose each of us just wanted to be on top, but I'm beginning to understand that's not what a marriage should be. Thank you for helping me to see that."

Peter stopped walking and held out his arms to embrace his mother. She wept openly on his shoulder.

"I once told your grandmother that I would try to do as you say. Obviously, I need to try harder, and I promise you I shall! And I promise you something else. I will discuss our conversation with your father and speak openly to him about my feelings.

Mother and son continued their sobering walk home, arm in arm. Peter Samuel wore a smile of satisfaction.

§

Anna Maria Bauer died in her sleep a week after her grandsons changed their name. Of course, Peter Bauer the businessman had changed his as well. Conrad thought it possible—but did not say so aloud—that his brother's and his sons' actions had broken her heart. He took another sip from the cup of bitterness.

Anna Maria had a long and fulfilling life at 85. She had rescued her family from lives that poverty, famine, and war would inevitably have shortened. She brought them successfully to America, confirming, like so many others in their circumstance, that country's promise.

Carolyn joined Conrad, their daughter, sons, and grandchildren, along with Louise and her family, Peter, and the Clarks at Anna Maria's funeral and burial. Conrad realized the significance of Carolyn's having gone with him to Griggs. Peter Samuel's 'intervention' had not been in vain.

PART VII
REMINISCENCE

29 A LONG SHOT

Conrad and Carolyn had talked occasionally about his retiring from the coal business. Throughout Conrad's working life, whether in Griggs or Sioux City, 'black gold' had been the nation's principal fuel, and people considered coal merchants were important members of the community. Now, in the waning years of Conrad's ownership of Bauer Coal, oil appeared on the verge of replacing coal.

Some in the coal business were thinking of switching to oil. Conrad had given the idea some thought, but he wasn't ready.

§

Three years had passed since Anna Maria's death. Carolyn had tried various methods to convey to her husband something—anything—of her desire to climb down from the cultural skirmishing that had beset their marriage from the beginning.

She remembered her mother's advice all those years ago:

'Just remember who you are and are not, young lady! Better climb down from that high horse of yours before you fall off!'

She struggled to overcome Conrad's impression that she cared little for the name 'Bauer' and its connotations—shoemakers and coal dealers—of a class beneath the DAR. Her letter to Anna Maria had been one of those efforts, but Conrad would not have known of it, and thus in appreciation of the sincerity in her attempt. She needed a more direct path to reconciliation.

Early in 1930 Carolyn believed she had come up with an idea—a long shot, certainly—that just might show her husband how much a cultural cease-fire meant to her. It was a long shot, that much she knew. Her plan required a nimble and credible introduction.

"Conrad?"

"Yes?"

"Do you think you could take some time away from your business?"

"How much time?"

"The children ... What am I saying? They're hardly children, each with his or her own families. Anyway, what I *wanted* to say was ..."

And here she slowed deliberately ...

"I wondered if you could take some time off ..."

"Oh?"

"I wondered if you took some time off, we could take a trip to Germany."

There! She'd said it. Carolyn knew she needed to let the idea of the trip sink in. She'd never hinted previously in any way that she'd like to visit Conrad's homeland. And she wasn't going to let something as inconsequential to her as declining stocks on Wall Street deter her.

He put down his knife and fork and stared at his wife. Then, he chose his words carefully, although he couldn't avoid sounding somewhat sarcastic.

"Maybe your business was hurt too badly by the crash?"

"No, no. The crash didn't touch us much. People still need coal ...

"But there are no 'Daughters' over there, you know."

"Please, Conrad. I'm trying to be serious. I'd really like to visit there. You say we can afford it. Maybe even Bierstadt."

"I don't have much feeling for Germany, Carolyn. After the war ... All of that. And now the politics are rather uncertain. Quite volatile, really. The government is weak primarily because of the inflation they started to subvert the Allied demands for reparations. Pay them off in worthless currency."

"My, it does seem you've kept up with things. I didn't realize."

"I just know what's in the papers, Carolyn, the same ones you read. Those from North Dakota are more informative."

"You mean I don't pay attention to news of Germany?"

"Do you?"

"I know about President Hindenburg. I know about the Communists, the National Socialists. I know what Adolf Hitler says about the Jews."

"Did you know that Peter admires Hitler?"

"Our Peter?"

"No! *My* Peter."

"Why?"

"His nationalism, especially his hatred of the Versailles thing. Germany should never have agreed to it."

"And the Jews?"

"He doesn't like them. Thinks Germany should rid itself of them … somehow."

"Oh, my goodness. What could that mean? What does Louise think?"

"As far as I can tell, she has no political views."

"You haven't said what you think of Hitler and the National Socialists."

"I don't have any political views, either. I keep my head down. Some people think I don't belong here, being German. That's something you don't have to worry about. You're lucky, Carolyn."

"Oh, Conrad, I so wish you could let go of thoughts like that. I learned to do it many years ago. Your sense of class, your Germanness keep me from being as close to you as I want. It hurts. Can't you try?"

"If my 'Germanness' bothers you, Carolyn, why do you want to go to Germany?"

"Because I think it will bring me closer to you. And when you see that I'm open to your homeland, you will stop keeping me at a distance. Besides, I think your 'Germanness' bothers *you*, not me."

He wondered what the DAR might think of her going, but he held his tongue.

"I'll make a deal with you, Carolyn. You get all the information you need for a stay of one month, and I'll be happy to escort you through a country *I don't know at all!* I'm sure by the time we leave, you will be more German than me."

She laughed, and he joined her. It was the first moment of levity on this subject she could remember. It made her happier than she'd been in years of their wrangling over class to see him finally make light of it instead of his usual sarcasm.

§

Carolyn studied and planned, then studied and planned some more until she finally worked out an itinerary for their month-long trip. They would travel by train. In each city they would see at least one art museum, stroll in a beautiful garden, sample regional food, beer, and wine, and talk with as many Germans as possible willing to indulge them and of whom they did not tire easily:

Bremen → Hannover → Berlin → Dresden (an absolute must) → Nuremberg → Munich (National Socialist 'capital') → Salzburg (absolute must) → Stuttgart (side trip to Bierstadt) → Frankfurt am Main → Köln (the cathedral) → Antwerp → New York.

§

Conrad booked 'Cabin Class' passage for two on the North German Lloyd (*Norddeutscher* Lloyd) passenger ship, the S.S. *Stuttgart* under the command of Capt. A. Winter. The ship embarked from New York on June 12, 1930, for Bremen by way of Cobh (County Cork) on the Irish coast, and Cherbourg.

"There she goes," Conrad noted aloud as the *Stuttgart* slipped quietly by the Statue of Liberty and out into open ocean. The vessel under his feet began to roll at once. He briefly recalled his last voyage on the Atlantic, which sent a sudden chill down his back. Then he returned to a tired theme.

"I don't know how long the ship will be in Cobh, Carolyn, but I do suppose you won't want to disembark in a country that fought like hell to get away from the oppressive clutches of your ancestors."

"You mean my DAR ancestors, don't you, Conrad? I thought this trip was to get past the place where I look down on your family and you mine."

But something else might have discomfited Carolyn: a shipload of Germans and German culture. All those *Auslandsdeutsche* returning home in answer to Herr Hitler's rallying cries. Yes, she'd grown up in North Dakota and married into a German family. But this was an immersion she couldn't escape even had she wanted.

There were many outright National Socialists and those who would be—all of them tiresome bores, she thought—aboard the *Stuttgart* that month, the 30th anniversary of her marriage. They dominated the salons with their steins, boisterous drinking, and nationalistic songs. *Gemütlich, Gemütlich, Gemütlich.* Too much *Gemütlich.* But she had wanted this trip and remained dedicated to its success, so she kept her counsel. And quite honestly, she was immensely curious about Germany and what was happening there. Should she overreact or react negatively, she wasn't sure her marriage would survive.

In their cabin, Carolyn found a folder having information about an afternoon music program. Privately, she viewed it as a peaceful way to get away from the crowds and noisy salons.

"Oh, let's go, Conrad, please! It will be calming and help set up our sea legs. I don't think I can eat later with all this excitement, everywhere."

§

If Carolyn needed another distraction, it came in the dining salon. Dinner choices that first night at sea must have seemed overwhelming ...

Featured Boiled Striped Bass, Roast Vierland Duck, and Vanilla Ice Cream, Sponge Pastry for Dessert.

Menu Items
Thursday, June 12, 1930
Dinner
(To Order)
Fresh Sea Shrimps in Mayonnaise
Sweet Pickles

Chicken Cream Soup Mogador
Consommé Jardinière
Consommé en Tasse
Boiled Striped Bass, Drawn Butter or Sauce St. Malo

Larded Saddle of Veal with Gravy
Cauliflower Polonaise /Nostitz Potatoes
Vol-au-Vent Frascati

Roast Vierland Duck, Apple Sauce - Simpson Salad with Lorenzo Dressing
Fresh Green Peas with Lettuce, English Style
Soufflé Lyonnais (ca. 10 Minutes)

Vanilla Ice Cream, Sponge Pastry
Assorted Cheese
Pumpernickel
Fruit in Season
Demi-Tasse
Sanka Demi-Tasse

From the Grill (ca. 10 Minutes):
Sirloins Steak, Horseradish Butter

Suggestion
Fresh Sea Shrimps in Mayonnaise
Consommé Jardinière
Boiled Striped Bass
Sauce St. Malo
Roast Vierland Dude, Apple Sauce
Simpson Salad with Lorenzo Dressing
Vanilla Ice Cream, Sponge Pastry

They would need to watch their weight!

30 GEMÜTLICH

Carolyn and Conrad disembarked in Bremen to find not one but two Germanys. Until the late 1930s, Germany successfully promoted itself as the ideal place to vacation, its smiling people overflowing with the familiar *Gemütlich* and eager to please. The land of Goethe and Beethoven had much to offer.

Conrad Bauer played the part of an interested husband, never suggesting in any way that art museums were something other than fascinating. They toured many such 'places' on their circuitous holiday.

After finding their footing in Bremen (Art Hall, Weserburg, and Paula Modersohn-Becker Museum) and Hamburg (Hamburger Kunsthalle), the serious attention to art and archaeological treasures began in earnest in

Berlin with the Pergamonmuseum, the Kaiser-Friedrich-Museum, and the Old National Gallery.

In Berlin, the couple experienced evidence of Germany's important and lasting contribution to the Modernist revolution, which in the late 19th century had begun to transform the European aesthetic sensibility. Amid the political and economic turmoil of the early 1920s, Germany's cultural and intellectual life flowered, docents told them.

The 'Weimar Renaissance' fulfilled the Modernist revolution. Its rejection of tradition perfectly suited the need of many Germans for new meanings and values to replace those destroyed by '14–18.' One of the 'new meanings' was the Bauhaus school of design. Bauhaus artists believed they were creating a new world through their painting, poetry, music, theater, and architecture.

Continuing from Berlin, they found that nothing thus far could surpass Dresden: the Dresden Castle, Old Master's Gallery, and the Zwinger Palace were just what Carolyn had hoped for on this trip. Then, beyond her curiosity about the Munich stronghold of the National Socialist Party, Carolyn adored the Alte Pinakothek and the Bavarian National Museum.

"Enough!" Conrad insisted finally. He wanted to be diplomatic about Carolyn's dragging him from one museum to the next, but his tone suggested otherwise. Typically, Carolyn chose the high road, which, in this case, would prove to be literally true.

"Oh, Conrad, please? Salzburg isn't far, and there's just one museum I have on my list. They say it's a lovely city; lots of good beer. I can visit the museum on my own while you find a nice, shady *Biergarten*. I'm sure you'll find some men there to talk with. Can you go to the station and get tickets? You'd be such a dear."

All this begging raised suspicions in Conrad's mind that after Salzburg, despite statements to the contrary, she'd never run out of museums. Carolyn continued her charm offensive.

"Conrad, I had no idea your country was so picturesque. You must be proud! Theater and music, delicious beer and sausages, the best universities in the world."

In Salzburg, each partner went his or her separate way. Two hours later, her tour finished, she found Conrad at a prearranged *Biergarten*.

"Would you like a beer to refresh you? He asked.

"No, I think a glass of *Weise Vein* would suit me better. Thank you, Conrad.

He summoned a buxom waitress and ordered the wine and another stein for himself. When she returned and politely set down the wine with a smile and *"bitte,"* Carolyn, exhausted, sighed and sunk back into her chair.

"Well, did you find some drinking companions? Some interesting discussions?

"Believe it or not, these people LOVE to talk. But I didn't find anyone who wanted to talk about art museums. All of it was about this fellow Hitler, who these people consider one of their own. I didn't realize he is Austrian!"

"What's his appeal?"

"Mostly, the Versailles Treaty and the German government's acceptance of whatever restrictions the Allies think of next. They hate that the Allies forced Germany to accept guilt for the war and then leveled exorbitant reparations. They see Hitler as someone who will get rid of the

Versailles restrictions and restore Germany's greatness and rightful place in the world ...

"They also hate the Communists and claim the National Socialists will never allow Bolshevism here. And they scapegoat Jews. I noticed whenever someone mentioned the Jews, my drinking friends turned red, as though they were about to explode."

"Oh, my goodness! I should never have left you alone. You had a difficult time."

"Difficult, yes, but informative. I won't soon forget those people or their politics ...

"Now, on another matter that is related to the importance of the National Socialists, we seem to have landed here during a serious economic depression led by business retraction and sky-rocketing unemployment ...

> The Bismarck *Tribune*, June 17, 1930 —
> Depression in Germany started with the stock market crash on Wall Street last October. Our investors began withdrawing their loans to Germany, loans that had been made in response to the crushing reparations payments imposed on Germany by the vengeful Allies, principally France.
>
> Prices on the German stock exchanges fell drastically last December. Business failures multiplied. Early this year Germany's second largest insurance firm collapsed along with the biggest banks. Unemployment now stands at three million. Germany's industry is working at no more than 50 percent of its capacity, and the volume of German foreign trade has fallen by two-thirds.
>
> The first critically important political effect of the economic crisis occurred in March when the government coalition fell apart over

> the rising cost of maintaining the unemployment program adopted in 1927. That will only increase the popularity of extremist parties in future elections, principally the National Socialists. The fall of the coalition along with declining incomes (failed banks) makes officials fear that German parliamentary democracy is dead ...

"And you know what, Carolyn? My companions today told me that Hitler had incontrovertible proof that all of this was due to Jewish control over banking and finance, and their desire to ruin Germany!"

§

Little wonder the trip had taken on a negative aura after Salzburg. The Bauers continued gamely on to Antwerp, but not even the stopover in Bierstadt, a faded memory to Conrad, also meant little to Carolyn. It's place in their lives, had there ever been one, ended somewhere on the North Atlantic in 1882.

The sobering passage home from Antwerp on July 25 was 'Cabin Class' as before, but this time aboard the S.S. *Lapland* of the Red Star Line, commanded by Captain H. Harvey. The captain prepared the *Lapland* for brief stops at Southampton then south to Cherbourg before setting out on the final leg to New York.

By then, the S.S. *Stuttgart* was a distant memory for the Bauers, but in the years *after* their voyage the ship had an interesting sojourn ...

> *The New York Times*, October 19, 1946—
> North German Lloyd chartered *Stuttgart* in 1936 to transport over 500 Jewish refugees to

> South Africa prior to a deadline the Nazis had set for that year. This was part of the Nazi's effort to promote Jewish emigration.
>
> Three years later *Stuttgart* and other vessels requisitioned for the purpose transported the Condor Legion from Spain back to Germany after the defeat of Republican forces by Franco's Nationalists who the Germans had supported with war materiel and troops (*Stuttgart's* share of the evacuation was nearly 800 men).
>
> The Germans commissioned the *Stuttgart* into the *Kriegsmarine* as *Lazarettschiffe C* in August 1939, and it served in Norway.
>
> *Lazarettschiffe C's* war ended on October 9, 1943, when American planes attacked it during a raid on Gotenhafen (Gdynia, Poland). Flames engulfed the ship, and the Germans towed it out of the harbor where it sank, full of wounded men, few of whom survived.
>
> The Wehrmacht War Crimes Bureau, tasked with recording all allegations and acts considered crimes against German soldiers, determined the attack on the ship had not been a war crime. True, the unarmed *Lazarettschiffe C* while at anchor had displayed Red Cross markings—under partial camouflage.

All this was much in the future as far as the Bauers were concerned. Probably just as well, considering what they had experienced of the relative innocence of Germany's politics in 1930.

31 TRANSITIONS

Conrad turned 65 in 1935 and Carolyn 66. In turn, Julie reached 35; John Charles, 32; and Peter Samuel 30. Each sibling had, in the same order, a husband, wives, children, and challenging lives.

The 'Bowers' and 'Bauers' of Sioux City via Griggs had proved proverbially fruitful. Julie, who always took an active interest in politics and society, completed courses at the University of North Dakota necessary for a high school teaching credential. At Grand Forks, she met and some months later married Bruce Hedman. Bruce took a sales job at Julie's grandfather's former pump business in Griggs, and Julie began teaching at Griggs High School. By 1935, they were the parents of two, Philip and Sofia, or 'Sofie.'

John Charles and Peter Samuel parlayed their Illinois B.A. degrees in business into a CPA (John) for a construction company, and personnel manager (Peter) for a sparkplug manufacturer. Each lived in a big city elsewhere in the Midwest.

Both brothers married women they met while at university. Bethany Williams became John's bride; they had one child, Anna. Peter and Elizabeth LaMar also had just one, Mila. John and Peter had explained to their wives and girls why they were the 'Bowers' and Grandma and Grandpa were the 'Bauers.' All thought the difference and its explanation much ado about ...

§

Conrad struggled to shake his conviction something had gone terribly wrong in his homeland. The visit five years earlier had scared him plenty about Germany's future. In that sense, the trip had defeated Carolyn's purpose. True, she believed it helped to know him better. But at what price to *his* peace of mind.

Perhaps the troubles began when Germans started calling it the 'Fatherland.' For the past five years, what he had seen and heard there haunted him, depressed him. If he had been scared before, now he was frightened. Perhaps it was it the demons who now ruled the place. But why should he care? For most of his life he'd had no thought of, or feeling for the place.

During a visit to Griggs after the trip—alone—he had talked to Peter and Louise about his impressions. They didn't seem to care or express worry. All they saw was that the National Socialists had restored the German economy and made the country respectable again—to some but not al—in international affairs. His siblings didn't believe the rest of the world cared very much about what went on there. None of their business ... None of their business about the Jews.

Conrad returned home even more depressed. Nothing he told them of his experiences or what had occurred since made any impression.

"We live in North Dakota, Conrad. It's certainly none of our business what happens over there, and no one over there gives a hoot about North Dakota."

§

A dark cloud hung over Conrad as he continued to contemplate the fate of his homeland. The trip to Griggs worsened his depression. Any psychiatrist would have cautioned against making decisions while in that state of mind, but Conrad had always been impulsive. He began seriously to consider retirement. It proved not to be a lengthy exercise.

On a Saturday morning after a busier-than-usual week in mid-November, when the cold had really settled in, he decided he'd had enough of the 'dirty' business. He was looking forward instead to Thanksgiving when he'd have his children and grandchildren to dote over instead of payroll and the petty grievances of customers and employees insisting on their 'rights.' Time to move on. No more whiny or angry calls from customers complaining their coal didn't burn 'right' or stunk up the house; could he come and get it. Nonsense like that.

Memories of those calls, old and recent, moved him to act quickly. His mind suddenly made up, he leapt out of bed, sort of, announced to Carolyn what he planned to do, and began making phone calls. It astonished even Conrad that before the end of the year he had a buyer, a conglomerate whose interest was not so much in coal as it was oil, the 'new kid on the home-heating block, so to speak. Those oil people didn't give a 'clinker's damn' about the coal, he had gathered. They'd sell the trucks to the sand and gravel folks or the state transportation department, most likely for use in highway repair. The oil people just wanted the property and no competition.

§

Conrad's decision pleased Carolyn … as soon as she got over the shock of its suddenness. What optimism she did have at his decision, which was not overwhelming, was based on her hope that it might lower the barrier between them. Still, a nagging question remained. Conrad stopped *working* in coal, but had that changed her *attitude* about someone who had?

From the beginning, the contrast in class and culture in their relationship had lurked like a dark shadow in the not distant recesses of Conrad and Carolyn's relationship. Occasionally, that shadow stepped forward, as it had with the trips back to Griggs. For the most part, however, the clash remained subliminal, and the lying-in wait continued. Each party realized the difference in their backgrounds had the potential to drive them apart—permanently. So, when Conrad sold the business, Carolyn didn't sound the trumpets. She celebrated silently. She'd won a battle—a big one in her mind. But would the war continue?

The truth about Carolyn Bauer? She lived in a bubble, a haven of sorts that her association with the DAR shielded. Protected in her view of what was and was not a proper class or culture, she never stepped back, so far as is known, to appreciate the business acumen and success of a 'coal dealer' without pedigree who had supported his family for decades. Coal, and that lowly 'coal dealer,' in Carolyn's quiet estimation, gave the Bauers of Sioux City a solid middle-class life and put their three children through college. No mean accomplishment.

§

In a photograph of the two in 1940, probably taken at their 40th wedding anniversary, they stood in their Sunday best. One might have expected Carolyn to cut a dashing figure, perhaps in the latest high fashion. And Conrad? Anything but *haut couture.*

So much for expectations! There they were, Carolyn in a serviceable, plain frock, thick beige stockings and black shoes—dowdy-looking really. And Conrad? Debonaire, looking as though he had just stepped out of a fine men's store in Sioux City after a fitting. His suede shoes set off by a tailored 3-piece suit with a sharp, unbroken trouser crease.

One must resist the temptation to comment on character from a single photograph. That said, the two septuagenarians appear not to like each other much. Carolyn is expressionless; maybe a slight smile trying to break out. Conrad looks away, his countenance that of an old grouch. It suggested he wished to be anywhere else. One must always be charitable. Perhaps it was the sun in their eyes.

§

"What will you do now?" she asked him in a manner that intimated she knew the answer. She didn't.

"Well, for starters I'm going to write the great German-American novel, and you will be my muse!"

"Seriously, Conrad. I can't have you under foot, wandering around the house all day. I have work to do, and you don't."

"Never fear, my love. I shall learn to cook, do the washing and ironing, and especially watch out for your feet!"

She had to suppress a laugh lest it encourage him.

"Oh, be serious, will you, Conrad Bauer? You will do none of that, and you know it."

"Then I'll write an exposé of the DAR. I'll reveal its deep, dark plan to emasculate the men of America, turn them all into coal dealers and shoemakers."

"Please don't say those things. It doesn't help."

§

That was the present. What of the future? Conrad Bauer never got around to writing that novel, learned to cook, do the washing and ironing, or unmask his own made-up plot by the Daughters of the American Revolution to turn the men of the United States into anything. But that did not end his disquiet.

PART VIII
SECOND-CLASS CITIZENS

32 A GOOD MAN

Stephen Kincaid rolled over in bed and gently swung his arm toward his wife's half. Empty. He raised up on an elbow to look, blurry-eyed, first at the bed and then around the room. No Amy. Then it came to him with the next breath. The smell of coffee. He heard the toilet flush.

Kincaid, or 'Kin,' her affectionate name for him, collapsed back onto his pillow, and closed his eyes. The next thing he knew, which could have been seconds, minutes, or hours later, someone was shaking him and calling him 'Honey,' all syrupy and soft-like.

His eyes fluttered open, and there she was. The girl of his dreams. His wife, Amy. His first thought, 'It's going to be a great day. The bad guys better beware!'

"Coffee's ready, Kin," she said softly but firmly."

"What time is it?"

"Six-thirty. We're running late, so you'd better shake it."

He did his bathroom chores quickly and efficiently, just he had at Quantico—toilet, teeth, and whiskers. But this was not 'shit, shave, shower, and shampoo,' which he'd learned to say about morning ablutions in the 'head' (Navy parlance for 'bathroom').

"Smells great, Honey," he purred as he came into the kitchen.

"You've got to fix your own bacon and eggs, Kin. I'm running late, too. I put everything out."

"Aren't you having any?"

"Fifteen minutes ago. I couldn't wait any longer. I said you were running late. I'll see you tonight."

'Well, shoot,' he thought, 'maybe not so great a day.'

§

Five years earlier, Stephen had wanted nothing more than to finish first in his class at the FBI Academy in Quantico, Virginia, return to Winona, Minnesota, and marry his high school sweetheart. He got one wish but not the other.

Amy Bowman, a cute and clever redhead—twice as clever as Kincaid, which everyone in their class of '37 knew. She, too, had two wishes, one of which focused on landing Stephen Kincaid in time; they had shared everything from chemistry class to the rear seat of his '36 Chevy coupe. Her other desire was selection as 'Teacher of the Year' at Bismarck High where she had taught chemistry the past two years. Like Stephen, she got one wish but not the other.

Amy knew 'Kin' to be a good man. She thought the FBI and the country were lucky to have him. But she had doubts about the FBI director, who she gathered through inference (clever, remember) was accumulating increased power from a compliant president of the United States.

The latter's weakness in dealing with Director Hoover concerned her, especially because of the assignments handed to her husband by the Bismarck SAC (Special Agent in Charge). She detested the idea of citizens using the FBI to help them pursue personal vendettas—to what end she could only imagine—against fellow citizens in the name of national security. The newspaper headlines and radio broadcasts breathless reporting events in Germany had begun to seem eerily familiar to Amy Kincaid.

"Kin, what do you think about these people who call the FBI's hotline with all these tips about so-called spies, and saboteurs, and the like? Don't you think many of those callers are just getting even with a neighbor or a relative over some trivial matter?"

"Honey, it's not my job to have an opinion about their motives. My job is to carry out orders. We must check out each one. Some are likely to be valid. What if we skipped one today and tomorrow that person blew up a factory? We just can't take that chance."

Amy listened but wrestled with his explanation. It did not comfort her, and her doubts led her to those questions she had about the relationship between Director Hoover and the president. A life-long Democrat, raised in a family that belonged to the Farmer-Labor Party of

Minnesota, she made a mental note to support someone other than Franklin Roosevelt in 1940. She had learned not to trust him.

33 THE INTERVIEW

Conrad Bauer, a couple of months shy of his 70th birthday, began his day slightly differently than Agent Kincaid. True, Carolyn was already up, and he could smell their breakfast. But he didn't move very quickly those days. It seemed every movement in getting out of bed played in slow motion. Creaky. Achy. His walk to the bathroom was slow and, when he got there, limited to one activity, not four at once.

Back in the bedroom, dressed only in his underwear, he pulled on a pair of jeans and snapped the suspenders over his shoulders.

"Carolyn!" he shouted. "You seen my slippers?"

"Don't you yell at me from another room, Conrad Bauer. You know how much I dislike it. And no, I haven't seen them."

"Sorry," he said sheepishly as he came into the kitchen, wearing them.

"Just where I left, 'em, I guess."

"Sit down, Honey. You want toast? ... Where are your glasses?"

§

Conrad's ambition for mastering the kitchen and washroom may have gone a cropper, but he did manage to stay out from under his wife's feet. Mostly what he did was track events in Europe—the war.

"Eric Sevareid says France is doomed, Carolyn. 'Collapse imminent.' Those are his words. Says so right here in the Bismarck paper."

"What does he know? What do the generals say?"

"Paper doesn't say. Churchill's over there. Maybe they're talking to him."

"What does that man in the White House say?"

"Same as always. He's not going to send our boys into a foreign war."

"Tosh!"

"Shhh ... Did you hear that, Carolyn?"

"Don't you shush me, Conrad Bauer! Hear what?"

"It sounded like someone at the door. I'll go."

Conrad shuffled toward the front door in his slippers and without his glasses. He looked through the small glass pane in the door at two men in suits and fedoras. He didn't recognize either. He opened the door.

"May I help you?"
"Mr. Conrad Bauer?"
"Yes."

Both men held up what appeared to be police badges.

"I am Special Agent Kincaid of the FBI. This is Special Agent Stanley Fisk."

Conrad squinted at the badges, but he couldn't read either.

"May we come in?" Kincaid asked.
"Who is it?" Carolyn called from the kitchen.
"FBI, they say. They want to come in."
"Well, invite them in and ask if they'd like coffee."

Carolyn, her curiosity peaking, started toward the door. Neither agent accepted her offer of coffee.

"Sir?" Kincaid said.
"Yes! Yes! Come in gentlemen."

The quartet seated themselves in the living room.

"What is this about?" Conrad asked.
"Do you know a Mr. Peter Bower of Griggs, North Dakota?" Kincaid began the questioning. He was unaware of Peter's name change.
"Yes, he's my brother."
"Do you visit him there?"
"Yes, of course."
"How frequently?"
"Oh ... How often, Carolyn?"
"My husband sees his brother two to three times a year."
"What do you talk about? Politics? His business? Your business? The weather?"
"Well, mostly we talk about family."

"Ever talk about Hitler and Germany? The war? President Roosevelt?"

"Yeah, all that ... but not the president. Why are you asking me these questions?"

"When did you come to the United States?"

Conrad paused, looking at Carolyn.

"I think it was 1882," he answered, finally.

"Were you naturalized?"

"What do you mean?"

"Did you become an American citizen?"

"Yes, of course he did," Carolyn answered.

"Ma'am, we'd like your husband to answer the questions."

"Don't you call me, 'Ma'am!' I'm no Madam!"

Both agents reddened.

"Of course. I apologize, Mrs. Bauer," Kincaid said and returned his attention to Conrad.

"Sir, did you become an American citizen? ... Were you naturalized? If you were, you should have a paper."

"He did it right away. Before he met me."

"Mrs. Bauer, please!"

Carolyn glared at the two men and left the room.

"Did you know your brother did not become an American citizen until 1914, when Germany started the first war?"

Agent Kincaid did not tell Conrad the FBI had received calls concerning Peter 'Bauer,' calls that raised questions about his loyalty to the United States. By inference, association, that disloyalty would also be Conrad's. Those calls only began during the period of France's hapless resistance to the Germans, which Conrad had just described to Carolyn.

"No, we never discussed that," Conrad replied. "I didn't have any reason to know or care when he became a citizen."

"Did you ever talk about that war with him?"

"No, I told you we never talked about any war."

"Here it is!" Carolyn shouted, returning to the living room. She thrust a paper in front of Agent Fisk.

Fisk quickly scanned the paper and handed it to Kincaid.

"Okay," Kincaid said a moment later. "It says you were naturalized in 1898."

"That's right, Mr. ... Uh ..."

"Kincaid, Mrs. Bauer."

"Like I was going to say, 1898, because that was the first time Conrad came to our house ... to court me!"

Kincaid and Fisk ignored Carolyn's proud non sequitur.

"Have you been back to Germany since you left, Mr. Bauer," Fisk asked.

"Yes, I believe it was in 1930."

"Why did you go there and for how long?"

"About a month. My wife wanted to get to know Germany because I came from there."

"Did you meet with family over there?"

"No, I don't have family there any longer."

"Did you talk about the political situation in Germany with anyone while there?"

Conrad and Carolyn looked at each other nervously, enough to increase Kincaid's suspicion of Conrad's disloyalty.

"Do you know it's a crime to lie to the FBI?" Fisk asked.

Conrad shook his head. He began to be frightened.

"I drank beer with some guys—once. They all liked Hitler. I didn't then, and I don't now!"

"How do you feel about Hitler now that he's started another war and is rolling over Europe?"

"Like I just said. I don't like him—or the French!"

Kincaid and Fisk exchanged a look.

"You do realize, don't you," Kincaid said, "that France is an ally of the United States, and your comment might suggest disloyalty to this country?"

Carolyn threw up her hands and stood.

"I don't want to be rude, but perhaps it's necessary. You gentlemen need to leave, now! Conrad?"

"Just a minute, Carolyn," Conrad replied. "I want to know if the FBI is going to charge me with disloyalty."

He turned toward the agents who had stood begun walking slowly toward the door.

"Well," he said. "Are you going to charge me with disloyalty?"

"Take it easy, Mr. Bauer. Headquarters will evaluate what you have told us. They will decide whether to charge you."

"If you clear me, are you going to report that."

"We don't report on people who are cleared."

"Ah, ha! So, you leave the impression with everyone that someone is guilty of disloyalty, even though you have cleared them," Carolyn reasoned. "What kind of justice is that? Who gives people like you the authority to ruin lives and then run home to your wives and children who will treat you royally and never suffer such treatment? How do you look at yourselves in the mirror every day and not throw up? How does a person restore their good name after you've dragged it through the mud? Isn't that just what someone like Hitler does?"

"I'd hold my tongue if I were you," Fisk warned Carolyn.

"I don't have to hold my tongue! I'm an American! I'm no German! she shouted and instantly regretted it.

Conrad glared at her.

"Good day. Thank you for your time, Mr. Bauer," Kincaid said as the pair closed the door behind them.

Carolyn broke into tears when they were gone.

"Oh, Conrad, I had to say something after what they told us about clearing people. My God!"

She slumped. Conrad wanted to take her in his arms, but he couldn't. 'I'm no German!' rang and rang in his ears.

§

"What's wrong, Kin? I can tell when something's bothering you."

He looked at her but said nothing for a while. She knew when to pull back.

"Amy, honey," Kincaid finally said during supper. A person told me something today … It made me wonder if I'm cut out for this job. I thought I was, but now I'm not sure."

"What on earth do you mean?"

Stephen Kincaid recounted what he could recall of the last few minutes of the Bauer interview.

"What do you see when you look at me after what I've told you?"

"I see a wonderful man, Steve Kincaid, a man doing the job he's paid to do—protecting your country."

Then Amy Kincaid said something that made her cringe inside, but she knew her husband to be a good, honest man, and she wanted to be supportive.

"Those people ... Were they immigrants? Those people had no right to say those things. They're not like us."

Then Stephen Kincaid said something that justified her faith in him.

"But they are, Honey. They're citizens like us. All of us have rights. I hope I'm not abusing them, that's all ... Some of the stuff we do ... I'm just not sure right now I could call those things 'patriotism.'"

34

PETER BAUER

"You won't find any firearms, gentlemen. No shortwave, either. No need to look under the bed."

"We must look, regardless. What about these magazines? They're in German, and many of them feature photographs of Hitler. Why do you have them?"

"I'm an American citizen. I have rights. We are not at war with Germany, are we? ... By the way, do you have a warrant to search for firearms and a shortwave?"

Lloyd Burrell and Donald Stacey, the special agents from the FBI field office in Bismarck, ignored Peter's insistence they produce a warrant. They understood him to be an American citizen, but their office had received several calls on a devoted line, messages, some hysterical, some hinting, some accusing him of disloyalty.

"You said you're an American citizen. Do you have proof of that?"

"I have a paper."

"I'd like to see it."

Peter left the room and returned a few minutes later, waving a paper.

"May I see it, please?"

The agent looked over the Certificate of Naturalization dated August 8, 1914.

A photograph—date unknown but perhaps associated with his naturalization—showed Peter to be unconcerned (oblivious?) with his appearance. He scowled at the photographer, perhaps because of the sun. For the occasion, he wore a wrinkled shirt and trousers, the latter so ill-fitting he needed suspenders to hold them up.

"When did you come to this country, Mr. Bower?"

"I believe it was in 1879."

"Why did you wait so long to apply for citizenship? You could have done it in five years. You waited 35. Why was that?"

"I had to work for a living. I had no time to do all they required. Learn English. Learn the Constitution, as you call it."

"What is your work?"

"I repair and sometimes make shoes. In the Old Country I was a master shoemaker. Here, not so much."

"Are you an educated man, Mr. Bower?"

"What do you mean?"

"How many grades did you finish—in school? How much schooling have you?"

"Here, I think you call it 6th grade. In Germany you learn all that by the 3rd grade, even the sons of shoemakers. Pupils over there learn more and learn quicker than here. So, six grades of schooling."

"So, you think Germany is a better country than America?"

"Did I say that? I don't think I said that, but you are writing it down regardless. Why? Have you been studying what the Nazis do? Am I to face the guillotine?"

"Don't get cute with us, Mr. Bower. It won't go well for you if you do."

"So, it *is* to be the guillotine."

"That's enough! I am placing you under arrest for disloyalty and subversion. Place your hands behind your back."

"Where are you taking me?"

"My partner will put you in our car so we can gather evidence without interruption. You'll have further interrogation in Bismarck."

"Don't you need a warrant for that? I never took the citizenship examination for 35 years, as you put it, but when I did, I read the Bill of Rights, a remarkable document, don't you think?"

"All right, if you insist, we'll take you to Bismarck, get a warrant from the judge, and return for the evidence. A local policeman will watch your home until we return."

"It isn't me who insists. It is our Constitution, which, I believe, you have sworn to defend. Isn't that right?"

Burrell and Stacey marched Peter to their waiting car and placed him in the back. On their return to the house, Stacey had something to say.

"Nothing more than a 3rd grade education? Maybe we should have gone to school in Germany!" he suggested half-seriously.

This did not amuse Burrell.

The two frustrated FBI agents rode in silence to the Bismarck field office. As soon as they had booked Peter, he mentioned another procedural right, conveniently or unintentionally overlooked.

"I'm entitled to a phone call. Please, where is the telephone?"

An agent picked up a phone from another's desk, walked it over to where Peter sat, and slammed it down in front of him. Peter smiled at the man with ill-disguised satisfaction and placed a person-to person call to Sioux City, Iowa.

35 A 'FIFTH COLUMN'

"How did it come to *this*?" Carolyn asked her husband when he hung up the phone. "Peter repairs shoes, for goodness's sake. He's 80 years old! He came to this country ... When?"

"1879."

"How could anyone possibly imagine he—or you for that matter—would be part of some plot to destroy this country! In all my life that's the most absurd thing I've ever heard anyone say. Tosh!"

"Peter said he needed a lawyer, Carolyn. He hoped I could help with that." He paused. "I did work with one when I had the business. I could ask him what to do."

Suddenly, Carolyn felt faint. She had been standing while Conrad and Peter talked. Now she decided to sit before she fell. She knew the answer to her question, 'How did it come to this?'

"Oh, Conrad, I'm so sorry!" she said once she'd regained some equilibrium. "It's all my fault!" she cried tearfully. "I insisted on that trip to Germany. I had no idea what seemed so innocent came to this. Then I said that awful thing about not being German. I'm so, so sorry. I said it in the heat of the moment; it wasn't meant. I don't know how to make it up to you both."

"Honey, you have nothing to make up. Shoe on the other foot, and I would have said I wasn't an American. The FBI would have come anyway. They're doing this all over the country, whether people went to Germany or not. It wasn't the fault of any of us. It's the times. All this super patriotism!"

Conrad came over to her armchair and sat on the arm. He put his arm around he shoulders and kissed the top of her head. They stayed that way for fifteen minutes, until she stopped crying.

She wiped her eyes and blew her nose.

"Honey," she said, looking up at her husband, "maybe there's a possibility other than the lawyer you were considering."

Conrad stared curiously at Carolyn, waiting for her to finish the point.

"First promise you won't get angry."

"I won't promise anything ahead of time. You know that."

"Okay. Well, my DAR chapter might be able to help with any legal or Constitutional issues. We Daughters do care about those things."

She expected him to explode. He didn't.

"We need help, Honey. I'll take it wherever we can get it."

"Do you mean that, Conrad?"

"Yes, I do. But let's call Julie before we do anything. She knows politics and history. I trust her. Do you think now's a good time?"

"I think so. I'll try while it's on my mind."

Carolyn dialed Julie's number.

"Mom! How are you?"

"I'm fine, Honey, but we've got a problem. The FBI was here, asking your father questions, and they have arrested Uncle Peter. Have you seen him lately?"

"About a week ago. Seemed fine. I took him a warm supper. What did the FBI want? My God!"

"Your father talked to him. The FBI had him at first, but they planned to transfer him to the county jail in Bismarck. They accused him of disloyalty, a threat to the security of the United States, if you can imagine. Possibly your father, too. He said they're targeting Germans all over the country."

"Father?" she exclaimed incredulously.

"Yes, Father," Carolyn repeated as though trying to convince herself of the truth of it.

Julie was silent a few moments. Then ...

"It's the 'fifth column,' Mother"

"Huh? 'Fifth column?' What in the world is that?"

"Many people think it's the reason for the rapid surrender of all those countries in Europe. This so-called 'fifth column' are a bunch of enemy sympathizers who propagandize, sabotage ... weaken the target country from within. Then, in this case, the Germans pour in from four directions, or columns. They meet little or no resistance because of the dirty work of the 'fifth columnists.' People here just can't imagine a country as powerful as France collapsing so quickly—or collapsing at all ... unless."

"This 'fifth column' sounds like treason to me."

"Yes, it is."

"So, the government thinks your father and Uncle Peter are traitors?"

"Yes, but they'd have to prove it before there's any real danger."

"Honey?"

"Yes, Mother?"

"Could you find some time to come down? Uncle Peter wants us to find a lawyer. I'm thinking of asking the DAR for help with that. We could use your advice."

Julie paused again.

"Have you talked to John and Peter Samuel about this? If not, I think you should. Bruce is working very hard right now, so I'd have to find a substitute for my classes and bring Philip and Sofie with me. Would that be okay if we could work it out? I can't promise anything."

"Oh, Honey, it would be wonderful! You know how grandparents are about grandkids. When can you make it?"

"Well, first I need to arrange for a substitute, and then I want to run over to Bismarck and make sure Uncle Peter is okay—for now, anyway. I need to do that tomorrow, so, how's the day after sound—or possibly the day after that? *If* I can find a substitute."

"That's fine. We'll wait, and we'll get in touch with the boys, okay?

36   'SEE YOU IN COURT'

Julie Hedman walked purposely to the door of the Bismarck FBI field office at 418 East Broadway Avenue, one of more than fifty field offices across the country.

Seconds after she rang the bell a voice came over the outside speaker.

"What's your business with the FBI?"

The voice struck her as that of someone hiding in a bunker, something she imagined she'd find in Germany, but something entirely inappropriate in a free country.

"I have questions about my uncle. You arrested him in Griggs a few days ago. He's elderly, and I'm worried about his health."

"Name?"

"My name is Julie Hedman. My uncle is Peter Bower."

A moment later she heard a buzzer at the door, and when she tried it, the door opened. An agent met her before the door closed behind her.

"Mrs. Hedman?"

"Yes?"

"How do you spell your uncle's name? There appears to be some confusion."

"B-O-W-E-R. He changed it from 'Bauer': B-A-U-E-R."

"I see. In any case, the FBI took your uncle to the Burleigh County jail. He will remain there until we've thoroughly evaluated his case."

"Might we sit somewhere. I'd like to explain some things about German immigrants and their challenges. My father is also from Germany, and your agents questioned him at his home in Sioux City. Has my uncle seen a lawyer?"

Apparently, the word 'lawyer' hit home. The 'doorman' looked around nervously, as if for help, and then signaled with his arm that she should follow him.

"Wait in this room for another agent."

She sat patiently for ten minutes, and then two men entered and introduced themselves.

"Miss ... Mrs. Hedman?" the tallest man began.

"Missus. Yes. 'Julie Hedman.'"

"Mrs. Hedman, I am Agent Burrell, and this is Agent Stacey. We questioned and arrested your uncle. He was most uncooperative."

"I don't mean to be presumptuous, but perhaps I can tell you some things that immigrants like my father and my uncle face in America."

"We can give you five minutes of our time, Mrs. Hedman."

"These men are loyal to the United States. I can't imagine you will find otherwise. But they are still partly German, and they can't help but feel a loyalty to their homeland. This does not mean they have any affection for the current regime. I can tell you unequivocally they do not ...

"Who is to say *when* immigrants have purged themselves of Old-World identities or that they *should*? Who is prepared psychologically for a war between one's homeland and the adopted country? That's a torment for them ...

"They have family ties to Germany. They felt the hurt of former countrymen over some provisions of the Versailles Treaty. They felt the hurt of former countrymen over postwar unrest, the struggle to survive the depression of the 1930s ..."

"We don't need a history lesson, Mrs. Hedman."

"You gave me five minutes. And maybe you do need to know a little history!"

Both. Agents glowered.

"Many German Americans, perhaps like my uncle, took pride in the prestige that Hitler restored to Germany and are reluctant to criticize him or *anything* German in public, reluctant to believe reports about the Nazis' treatment of the Jews, and reluctant to react to the dangers of American Nazis—the Bund. Before Hitler turned to conquest, these men admired his economic successes."

"Are you nearly finished?" Agent Burrell asked impatiently.

"Yes, thank you. Just a moment more of your time, please. For all I just pointed out, they have paid a price, and will continue to do so: the lingering doubts about their integrity, loyalty, and rightful place in America—much of it left over from the domestic hysteria accompanying World War I, as I'm sure you realize …

"They are also paying a price, again as you know, for reports about their lives in Germany and ongoing contacts there, for association with ethnic organizations and people of German ancestry in the United States, for the newspapers and magazines they read, statements they made to informers and agents such as yourselves that seemed disloyal, and self-incriminating, and ill-considered."

It seemed from their stone-cold looks that none of what she said made any impression.

"Do you wish to visit your uncle?"

"Yes, of course!"

Julie was a bit stunned. Maybe they just wanted to be rid of her.

"I'm writing out a visitor pass for you at county lockup. Just show it at the door."

"Who's in charge of releasing him?"

"That will be up to headquarters in Washington."

"Isn't there a limit to how long you can hold him he without filing charges? I can ask a lawyer."

"We have filed charges, Mrs. Hedman. We're holding him without bond as a threat to national security."

Julie was stunned.

"My uncle, age 80, a retired shoemaker and American citizen is a threat to national security? Seriously? Do you expect any judge to believe that? He must have sassed you pretty good, because I'm sure you've got no evidence that'll stand up in court."

Both agents shifted their feet nervously.

"Here's your pass, Mrs. Hedman. The man who saw you in will see you out."

"I'll be seeing you gentlemen in court ..."

"There won't be any court," Stacey turned slightly and shouted over his shoulder, interrupting Julie in mid-sentence.

"... when you get to tell the judge how you beat up an old man on a slow day!"

Julie either didn't hear Stacey, or she ignored what he said about court. But once outside she had time to reflect. Now, his shouted words worried her. What could he have meant? It seemed ambiguous. What would she say to Peter and to her father?

37 THE JAIL

"Hello! Mother?"
"Julie? Where are you? Are you still coming here?"
"I'm still in Bismarck. I found a substitute. I'll come down after I've seen Uncle Peter."
"Alright, Dear."
"May I talk to Father?"
"Yes, of course."

§

"Julie! Have you seen Peter?" Conrad asked at once.

"Not yet. I talked to the agents who arrested him. They listened to what I had to say, sort of, but that was it. They took him to the county jail. When I ring off, I'm going there to see him."

"Alright, Honey. Let us know how he is."

§

Julie took a cab to the county lockup on Thayer Avenue.

At the door, she showed her pass but met resistance.

"Look, lady, the FBI stuck him in here, and they're the ones to get him out. You got proof he's your uncle?"

"Not with me, no. Are you telling me it's your policy to require proof of a blood tie before a person can see an inmate? I'm not trying to get him out. Not yet anyway. I want to see your policy about visitors in writing, and I want to speak to your superior. A judge might take a dim view of your behavior."

The man disappeared down the hall, and five minutes later another man walked up to Julie.

"You have a pass from the FBI?"

Julie showed him the pass.

"Follow me," he said and walked back down the hall with Julie trailing behind.

The man, who had not introduced himself but who Julie assumed was the superior she had requested to see, opened successive doors, finally revealing a row of barred cells.

"Your uncle is in number 3. I'd like you to forget what happened earlier," he said before walking away. "I've dealt with that situation, and I apologize for it."

§

Julie walked along the tier of cells to Peter's. The space behind the bars, which she estimated was about ten by six feet, had an open toilet, a sink, a stool, and a cot that hung from the wall by chains at either end. Peter Bower was asleep on the cot. She wasn't sure she should wake him but decided she must, to encourage him and get information about the FBI confrontation.

"Uncle Peter," she whispered. He didn't budge, so she raised her voice slightly.

He sat bolt upright, clearly disoriented. Finally, he twisted around and peered toward the bars.

"It's about time," he grumbled. Clearly, he thought someone had come to let him out.

She could see he needed a shave. His thick white hair stood out in every direction. And he smelled. She wondered if he had urinated in his clothes.

"Uncle Peter, it's me, Julie, your niece."

"Julie? What are you doing here?"

Peter got up and walked to the bars.

"I'm trying to find a way to get you out, but the FBI says you are a threat. They're quite adamant on that point … and stubborn. Have you seen a lawyer?"

"No! he shouted. The 'Federal Bastards of Inquisition' have thrown away the key. They said I am to meet with a hearing board that may strip me of citizenship and deport me."

"Back to Germany? In the middle of a war? Did they say what evidence they have of your danger to the United States?"

"No. At my house they saw a newspaper and magazines in German. I gave then a good piece of my mind. Would that be 'evidence'?"

"I'm not a lawyer, Uncle Peter, but I don't see how one could construe that as evidence. Some people just have thin skins. Now, what do you need? Are you warm enough? I'll ask the sheriff if I can bring you something before I leave town."

"I could use a jacket. Where are you going?"

"To see my parents in Sioux City. They are concerned about you, of course. We're going to find a lawyer, so, you mustn't worry. Okay?"

She smiled and he nodded. She made her way to the sheriff's office to ask about some necessities.

"My uncle is elderly. He needs to clean up and put on fresh clothes. He also needs a jacket for warmth. Do you provide those things? Or do I?"

"There should be toiletries on the sink. We'll make sure he gets washed, and we can put him in a fresh prison shirt and trousers. The jacket or coat is on you. Just drop it off here. We'll see that he gets it."

Julie found a thrift clothing store two blocks from the courthouse. She bought a fleece-lined Mackinaw and returned it to the sheriff and backtracked to the bus station and eventually boarded for Griggs. Fortunately, the bus service ran a schedule that passed through Griggs about every hour.

Bruce had the children fed, packed, and excited for inclusion in such an important mission. The three waited at home until it was time for the train to Sioux City. Bruce kissed his children and wife. A soon as they took their seats, the children fell fast asleep. Then Julie closed her eyes, so exhausted she hadn't seen her husband waving goodbye from the platform.

38 THREATS

The weary travelers didn't arrive in Sioux City until around 9 P.M. Julie's mother was still up, but Conrad had gone to bed around five. Normally, both of her parents would have retired at the same time, but Conrad seemed especially tired.

The news that the government might strip Peter of his citizenship and deport him to Germany had shaken Conrad to the core. He told Carolyn he hadn't felt so tired in all his life. She encouraged him to go ahead to bed. It would be okay; she would wait up for Julie and the children.

They didn't bother to knock. The children were so excited and tired of sitting they burst into the house, their mother trailing behind.

"Come, you two! Give your old Granny a big hug."

Philip and Sofie rushed to Carolyn, who nearly toppled over as she swept them into her arms. Hugs and kisses over, the children set out to explore the house.

"You stay out of that cookie jar! You hear me in there!"

Distant giggling ensued. Carolyn and Julie smiled.

"It's so wonderful to see the three of you. I hope Bruce won't be too lonely."

"Oh, he'll love having a little peace and quiet for a change, Mother."

Both smiled again, knowingly.

"Julie, if you're not too tired, take the kids up then come back down and tell me briefly about Peter," Carolyn said to her daughter as Julie took off their coats and placed their suitcases at the foot of the stairs. "We can talk in more depth in the morning when your father is up. The news about Peter hit him quite hard, so he went up early."

"Well, briefly, there isn't much more to say than what I explained over the phone. He's to have a hearing to decide whether he should keep his citizenship. If he loses it, they'll deport him. He says that's what the FBI told him ...

"I got him a jacket because he complained of being cold. His hygiene has been terrible, so I persuaded them to get him washed and put him in fresh, clean clothes. Let's do talk more in the morning. I'm very tired, emotionally and physically. Back and forth to Bismarck, and then the long trip from Griggs. The children were so excited on the train."

"I can imagine," her mother replied. "Do go up now, Honey. We'll talk more in the morning. I have an idea."

"If Father's awake, please say goodnight for me."

"Yes, of course,"

§

The noise of rambunctious grandchildren woke Conrad around six the next morning. When he came downstairs, they rushed to embrace him, which turned into the three of them laughing and wrestling on the floor.

"Careful of your old Opa," Conrad cautioned. He used the German for 'Grandpa' because he had begun to let them hear and understand German. Carolyn and Julie did not object. What Bruce thought isn't known; he wasn't asked for his opinion and wisely avoided the subject.

Conrad finally managed to extricate himself from the children's grasp with deft moves of his own and wandered into the kitchen where he found Carolyn and Julie preparing breakfast.

He gave Carolyn a peck on top of her head, which Julie understood to be their way in the morning, and then took Julie in his arms and kissed her cheek.

"You saw Peter?"

"Yes. We must get him out of there, Father, but let's feed the children first and then talk.

§

"I have an idea," Carolyn said. "I'll contact my DAR chapter and ask for legal support. I'm sure they'll have a lawyer or two who can get Peter released."

"But he'll still have that hearing," Julie reminded them.

"I'm sure the lawyer will be able to get him out on bail of some sort and defend him at any hearing."

Another situation worried Julie.

"Are you clear of suspicion now, Father?"

"Apparently. But you never know these days. People are so panicked by what's happening across Europe."

"Are we agreed, then, on a strategy?" Carolyn asked.

Conrad and Julie nodded.

Late that afternoon Carolyn told Conrad and Julie that the DAR had recommended a lawyer. She arranged for the family to meet with Rodney Allen after he had traveled to Bismarck and interviewed Peter.

When Allen returned to Sioux City, he did not have encouraging news.

"I couldn't find any way to get him released before the hearing," Allen told them.

"Is there a date for the hearing?"

"Three weeks from this Thursday, in Bismarck. The government has charged Peter Bower with subversion and a threat to national security—in short, disloyalty. The government attorney filed a formal complaint on the basis that Peter's citizenship oath in 1914 was 'false and fraudulent' and he 'did not in good faith intend to renounce absolutely and forever all allegiance and fidelity to Germany' ...

"If the hearing board finds him guilty of perpetrating a fraud by taking an oath of loyalty to the United States, it may result in his being stripped of his citizenship and interned. Apparently, FBI Director J. Edgar Hoover is pushing these prosecutions so he can have men and women like your brother-in-law put away. He seems a very vindictive man. The agents didn't say that directly, but they hinted."

39 PROSECUTION

The hearing in Bismarck did not begin well for Peter. The court consisted of a prosecution lawyer, three judges—a tribunal—and Peter's defense lawyer.

The tribunal listened intently, as did the Bower family, to a searing and damning recitation of Peter's alleged acts of disloyalty and subversion.

The prosecution lawyer opened with an FBI agent other than the two who had engaged Peter at his home in Griggs. As evidence, the agent swore to a series of statements to which he attached numbers, statements allegedly made by Peter and provided to the FBI by informants:

1. 'The working class in Germany is much better off than in America.'

2. *'Defendant made many pro-Nazi statements.'*
3. *'Defendant told an anonymous informant that in Germany in 1937 the people were happy and had plenty of work and food. Conditions there were a lot better than when Germany had a democracy.'*

The prosecutor waved some papers at the tribunal. They showed, he said, that other informants claimed the defendant made 'pro-German' comments and had been 'very friendly' with two people already under Bureau surveillance.'

Allen rose to demand copies.

"Are these alleged statements by the defendant sworn to?" he continued.

"They are not," came the prosecutor's answer.

"Your honor, please!" Allen pleaded with the tribunal.

"In a proceeding such as this, Mr. Allen, the tribunal does not require sworn statements. You should know that."

The prosecutor then called Peter to the witness chair.

Peter admitted he had hoped for a German victory, but only 'for the sake of the German people.'

Did he make a distinction between the German people and the Nazi government?

"No," he replied.

Would he accept the Nazi government if it would bring victory for the German people?

"No," he replied again.

He did not hope for a German victory, Peter had told the agents who interrogated him at home, only the welfare of the German people.

Then, the prosecutor pressed Peter to answer what he believed would sink the old man.

"Everything being equal, do you hope Germany wins the war?"

Peter exploded. "Are you crazy? America is not at war with Germany! I am an American and I am a German. Were America to go to war with Germany, I would not wish either to win because that would mean the end of the other ...

"If the current war continues, and the United States joins, it will mean the end of my homeland. If the current war continues and the United States joins and Germany wins, it will mean the end of the United States. How would you feel in that circumstance? Is that why you dragged me in here to answer in the presence of these gentlemen? No one ever asked me a stupider question. Ever!"

Undeterred, the prosecutor maintained a confident air.

"The government rests, Your Honors."

40 DEFENSE

"Counselor?" the presiding judge said, casting his gaze on Allen.

Rodney Allen began his questioning of the FBI agents who prepared the indictments against Peter. They admitted they had little expert knowledge about the Germans on which to base their conclusions. Each file, such as Peter's—and presumably Conrad's as well—included the names of people who were *not* initially under suspicion.

"Were *they* dangerous, too?" meaning those not initially under suspicion.

"Unclear," was their answer.

"Then how did you resolve them?"

"We had two choices. Either assume their guilt by association or ignore the connection altogether, which proved impossible. In the end, the department set up an alphabetical index of all mentioned individuals, briefly noting their activities."

"Wasn't Peter Bower's a case that lacked clarity, as you say?"

"We concluded his disloyalty was clear."

"I beg to differ," Allen replied.

"I show you a document that says, and I quote, 'The Department of Justice's research showed how difficult the knowledge was of belligerent nationals in this country, *despite* extensive FBI investigations. This shortcoming led the department to conclude that *the FBI's role was a rather poor commentary on the security mindedness of the United States.*' Would you care to comment?"

In turn, the agents did not wish to comment, they said.

"Now, I show you another department letter in which one of your lawyers wrote, and I quote, 'the confidential FBI information in suspect files was *hearsay in nature and not admissible as testimony in a judicial proceeding.* Nonetheless, that department lawyer believed the Bureau must use the information because the government had not confined dangerous people.' Would you care to comment?"

In turn, the agents on the witness chair did not.

"Continuing with the same document, the same department lawyer offered a cynical solution for the problem. To quote: '*All evidence presented in the investigative reports, no matter its quality, was to be considered presumptively true, but that from the accused untrue*' ...

"Is it your position before this tribunal that the evidence I have just presented on *behalf of the accused*, and which by any reasonable measure cries out for the innocence of the accused, is *presumptively untrue* based on the statement I have just read to you? Do you care to comment?"

"Where did you get those documents?" one of the embarrassed agents demanded.

"Would you care to examine them? I have prepared copies."

The agent accepted the copies from the clerk and began looking them over but not really studying them.

"These are classified documents, Mr. Allen. How did you come by them?"

"If you look carefully, you will see a small stamp in red that says, 'Declassified.'"

"Humph," he muttered. His cursory reading had betrayed him.

"There is more, gentlemen."

Rodney Allen continued to read from the internal Justice Department documents.

"Later, a department lawyer and his assistant plotted their trial strategy in case a prisoner filed suit. I quote: *'Object strenuously all the way along,'* and at the close, move to strike all the plaintiff's evidence. Ignore everything' but two issues: the attorney general had the power to denaturalize and intern, and, logically, he could not be wrong'* ...

"Would any of you care to comment?"

In turn, the agents did not.

Allen then addressed the Court.

"May I continue, Your Honors?"

The chief judge, wearing a look of exasperation, waved his hand in a flip manner that signified 'yes.'

"Your Honors, continuing with the same document: 'The department should argue that the attorney general acted in the knowledge that *the FBI had investigated, and he should not, could not, challenge the FBI's accuracy. The question of loyalty is irrelevant. Defend the FBI's authority, period. Do not stoop to combat the evidence*' ...

Allen stared at the witnesses.

"Would you care to comment?"

In turn, the agents did not.

Allen again addressed the Court.

"The witnesses are unresponsive, Your Honors."

The judge in command of the hearing, in a voice dripping with irritation and menace that flummoxed Allen, who believed he had exposed the prosecution's duplicity, bellowed, "The Court is aware, counselor. You are skirting with contempt. Now proceed with your case!"

Chastened, Allen turned back to the agents who were smirking.

"Now, gentlemen, I ask you the following. Shouldn't FBI apprehensions be based on dangerous or hostile *activities,* not simply allegations that a subject sympathized with Germany? ...

"Many Americans, more influential than the ones under suspicion, have continued to express views harmful to the objectives of the United States: Charles Lindberg, for example. What should happen to him, or others like him? ...

"Either the entire group of such outspoken citizens is dangerous and are also guilty of the charges leveled against my client—a citizen—or, as a class, they are *not* a threat. It makes little sense to pick people at random, as the FBI has done. Isn't that true?"

The agents all shrugged.

Because the agents refused to answer any of his questions, Allen believed the tribunal had coached them ahead of the hearing; the 'judges' would not force them to comply.

Allen thought for a moment, and then took a huge risk.

"Have you 'gentlemen' met with members of the Court prior to today's hearing?"

The prosecutor leapt to his feet.

"Your Honors ..."

Before he could finish his objection, one of the three board members cautioned Allen.

"The Court warned you earlier, counselor. Any further attempt to cast aspersions on this Court will result in your being cited for contempt. Now, do you have anything else of relevance, Mr. Allen?"

"The Court leaves me no choice. The defense rests, Your Honors." Allen slapped the documents down onto his table in disgust.

Two hours later the trio of judges returned to the hearing room. They did not leave the accused and his family in limbo.

"We find the defendant guilty. This verdict was not a close call. Two board members voted guilty and the third, who voted against the majority, issued no dissenting opinion ...

"Nothing offered by the defense, while we agree it does not speak well of certain actors within the Justice Department, and for which there may be no excuse, none of it refutes the evidence presented against Mr. Bower. The defense made no attempt to challenge the credibility of prosecution witness statements, a fact that reinforces their testimony. It is now the responsibility of the Justice Department to decide the fate of Mr. Peter Bower."

The principal judge banged his gavel on the table.

"I declare this hearing adjourned.

Allen jumped to his feet as the tribunal rose to leave the room.

"We appeal, Your Honor."

The three judges stopped and turned toward Allen.

"That is your right, Mr. Allen," the lead judge replied. "However, based on the evidence presented at this hearing, I don't foresee success, but it is certainly your right to appeal."

Julie caught up with Allen as he left the courtroom.

"Why didn't you challenge the witnesses against my uncle?"

"I'm very sorry, Mrs. Hedman, but you can't cross examine a piece of paper. We still have the appeal, which I will file tomorrow, first thing."

"The Court must have known, Mr. Allen, did it not?"

"Of course. That's why we will win on appeal. Do not worry. Your uncle will have justice."

Julie watched him walk away, then turned back to her waiting family.

41 THE APPEAL

Three weeks later, Sinclair Halstead, an associate justice of the North Dakota supreme court, to whose jurisdiction Allen had directed Peter's appeal, issued his verdict. His judicial liberalism was well known among legal circles in North Dakota, where any evidence of liberalism was always suspect and readily castigated in newspaper editorials and other weapons of communication by sometimes unpleasant-sounding conservatives.

In defiance of North Dakota convention, however, four men trumped conservative opinion and saw to it that Sinclair Halstead took a seat on the Court as an associate justice. The four were: a popular president; a Democratic governor whose election was an anomaly in North Dakota; the recommendation of United States Supreme

Court Associate Justice, William O. Douglas; and Adolf Hitler.

Justice Halstead began reading his verdict with a warning to the government. It raised the hair on the back of Allen's neck and sent a chill down his spine:

> 'Sadly, in the case of the United States v. Mr. Peter Bower, this court finds it necessary at a time in our history, when the freedom of every citizen may eventually be at stake, to comment on the government's action against one of us, which was an action against all of us.'

Justice Halstead glared at the men seated at the prosecution table as he spoke. Indeed, with nary a glance at the sheaf of papers in front of him, he rarely took his eyes off the prosecution. Later, some who had been in the room said his stare could have frozen a block of ice. Halstead continued:

> 'No one told Mr. Bower he could not hold or express certain political beliefs and still be 'attached to the Constitution.' On the contrary, the government presumed Mr. Bower understood the meaning of the words, 'Congress shall make no law ... abridging the freedom of speech....' Had Mr. Bower not been an American citizen, 'It must be regarded as constitutionally settled that each liberty specified in the First Amendment ... is a liberty which is secured by the due process clause of the Fifth Amendment to all persons without regard to citizenship.'

Carolyn's pulse raced. Halstead read on.

'Advocacy of ideas or actions falling 'short of incitement,' or lacking 'exhortation to immediate violence or crime,' were not justifications to cancel free speech where nothing showed 'the advocacy must be acted on at once.' The government did not allege that Mr. Bower's statements, however heartfelt but misguided, created a 'clear and present danger' ...

'When Congress wrote the naturalization and immigration laws, it had in mind only the prohibition and naturalization of 'anarchists, political assassins, and polygamists,' not persons advocating an attachment to homeland or any other political philosophy ...

Suddenly, a disturbance at the prosecution table interrupted Halstead's reading. The prosecutor, who saw the direction of the justice's decision, looked at the justice in disgust as he noisily stuffed his briefcase with papers that lay in front of him. Finally, his briefcase stuffed, the man sat back with a deep sigh and folded his arms across his body, never shifting his gaze from Halstead. Justice Halstead returned the man's look of disgust with that withering glare of his own and continued his summation, which he had clearly memorized:

'It is understood ... It is understood,' he repeated, continuing to glare at the prosecutor for added emphasis, his voice louder. *'It is understood in the Constitution that a Nation which is strong enough to proclaim the individual liberties of the First Amendment is strong enough to apply and enforce and preserve them....*

They are strong enough to endure both war and peace ...

'In its finality, this action, one of the most ironic I have ever confronted in a long career, intended to penalize the defendant on the ground he was not 'attached to the principles of the Constitution' because he exercised the rights guaranteed to individuals in the declaration of those principles! In a crisis abroad to preserve the liberties set out in those principles, it would be strange indeed to deny them to a man for their exercise when we were not at war and under conditions where no clear and present danger is asserted to exist ...

'The appeal is sustained. Mr. Peter Bower is once again a free citizen of the state of North Dakota and of the United States.'

The audience stood as one and applauded. Conrad smiled broadly; Carolyn began to cry. Peter stood, somewhat bewildered, and Julie, barely able to hold herself together, took him in her arms.

"It's fine, Uncle Peter," she whispered. "It's a fine day."

He looked up at her and broke into a smile as broad as his brother's.

PART IX
SWANSONG

42   GRIGGS

"Carolyn?"

"Yes?"

"I need to spend some time with Peter. He's over 80, and I don't know how much longer we'll have him."

"Is he ill? Did he ask you to come up?"

"No, he's not sick as far as I know, and he didn't ask for me. But I think the suspicions leveled at him, his time in jail, an American citizen for God's sake! That and the hearing took a lot out of him, mentally and physically."

"Of course. I understand all that. But shouldn't you have him here for a rest instead of your going up there?"

Despite their history of her refusal to return to Griggs, she *still* wanted to argue against his going. She had this weird, gut feeling that if he went back to Griggs, she might never see him again. It was irrational, she knew, but there it was. She decided to keep a positive outlook, to hold her tongue, to keep a promise to Anna Maria. She didn't understand it wasn't always about her.

"Don't you want me to go with you? Before you answer, I realize how ironic that statement must seem."

"Carolyn, ironic doesn't begin to explain how it sounded. We've been married 40 years, and all that time you never went back with me. You even told Mother when Marta and Billy died that you intended to change, but you didn't. Do you have any idea how *not* ironic that is?"

"I have thought a great deal about it, Conrad."

She paused, her face turning sorrowful.

"Maybe we were just not meant to be. Think about it. It seems so improbable to have happened."

"Improbable, yes. But here we are because we love each other, always have—I hope always will—and that's made the difference."

"I never wanted you to think I wouldn't go back to Griggs because of our different backgrounds ..."

"But you *have* resented my background, whether *I* thought you did or not. I've held my tongue, but it's a wedge between us."

"Listen, Conrad. It's also true, is it not, that you have always, deep down, resented *my* background. Occasionally, you have made snide remarks about the DAR. But just remember, the DAR got us Mr. Allen, who did a masterful job at the hearing."

"Let's establish a truce and call it a draw, okay. We're too old with too much at stake to keep revisiting each other's backgrounds. I think we settled everything forty years ago."

Carolyn's face turned pink.

"You are a naughty boy, Conrad Bauer."

§

At breakfast the next morning Conrad again brought up the idea of his going to see Peter.

"You realize, don't you, Carolyn, that Peter and I have never spent any time together since you and I left Griggs?"

"Yes, of course."

"So, we have a lot to talk about, especially with what's been going on in Germany."

"Do you mean the war, or the war and other things?"

"The latter."

"Shouldn't you also share those thoughts with your children?"

"First Peter, then the children … I feel so silly calling them children. Isn't there another word for them?"

"Their names? Julie, John, and Peter?"

Conrad packed his paisley carpetbag one more time and boarded the train to Griggs.

§

At the station in Griggs, Peter's appearance shocked Conrad. He had aged considerably since his incarceration and hearing. Pale and frail-looking, his upper body bent forward from the waist as though he had developed a case of osteoporosis. His shirt and trousers needed ironing. He wore no belt; instead, he used a safety pin in place of a top button. The older man hadn't shaved for several days, and when they embraced on the platform, Conrad smelled urine.

Conrad's eyes misted over, and his vision blurred. His mind flooded with memories of his brother—a different brother. He began to deliberate how to persuade Peter to take better care of his hygiene, while not suggesting he was incompetent to do so. But he knew that mere persuasion was a dodge, a tactic employed to let himself off the hook so he could return home.

When they got to Peter's small house, the evidence of his brother's failing overwhelmed Conrad. The stifling airlessness meant windows were never open. Conrad quickly saw the threats to Peter's health: the odors; the unmade bed with sheets that needed washing; the sink full of dirty dishes; the opened cans of food; clothes scattered about; evidence of a cat or cats; and on and on.

"Peter, do you mind if I look for someone to do a little house keeping? Not much. Just a little."

"Who? I'm doing fine by myself. Is that why you came up?"

That left Conrad flummoxed, but before he could come up with a credible answer, Peter collapsed onto a chair, the only one in the living room free of clutter and began to quietly sob.

Clearly, Peter could no longer care for himself. That was an unavoidable truth. Could he, somehow—should he—continue to live alone?

Conrad did some minimal straightening and shelving, enough so anyone could move around comfortably, without stepping on or over clothes and dishes.

"Peter, I'm going over to the newspaper office to see if I can find someone to help out here."

Peter smiled weakly.

Instead of the newspaper office, Conrad went to Western Union and addressed a telegram:

> Mrs. Carolyn Bauer
> 367 Perry St.
> Sioux City, Iowa
>
> Peter ill. Unable to care for himself. Need your help. Please come. Conrad.

Carolyn must have wondered why he'd never said 'need your help' regarding her presence in Griggs.

A day later, which was a Friday, he received a telegraphed reply:

> Arriving 4 o'clock train Friday. Carolyn.

Conrad met Carolyn at the station. The changes in the town astonished her. Before she could do anything, she needed to reorient herself.

"Conrad, please take my things to the hotel ... Did you get us a room? I'm sure there isn't one at Peter's. I'm going to look for a beauty parlor and ask the clients if they know someone we could hire to help at Peter's."

"There's one called 'Betty's' over on North Pearl. Try it."

Carolyn's take-charge approach impressed Conrad—he hadn't yet booked a room—and he readily agreed to follow her instructions.

§

Carolyn found the salon straightaway.

BETTY'S

The name, presumably the proprietor's, appeared in script on each of two large windows flanking the door to the beauty parlor. That was it. Clearly, no woman in Griggs needed more information than a single word.

Carolyn scanned the interior as she entered. One woman was receiving a perm under the ministrations of a permanent wave machine. The other customers sat in rows either of sinks, hooded dryers, or against the wall flipping—snapping—through the pages of movie magazines, or weeks-old copies of *Time*, *Look* or *Life*. Some of them chomped on gum.

The few stylists at work all wore plain white dresses and similar hair styles.

'Betty's' clients, the ones who had removed their drying hoods, were laughing and chatting.

A cash register with a crank sat on the counter to Carolyn's right as she closed the door

A woman who Carolyn assumed was the owner came forward. Carolyn introduced herself as Peter's sister-in-law and explained her purpose. It was a good way to break the ice. Nearly every woman having a wash or chatting had done business with the cute little shoemaker.

'Betty' announced Carolyn's request to her clients.

"You know what?" piped up one client who had lifted the dryer from over a head covered with curlers. "Why don't you put up notes on bulletin boards over at the high school? I'll bet you'd get plenty of responses."

"That is such a great idea!" Carolyn replied enthusiastically. "Any of you have daughters—sons!—who might be willing?"

"Where are you staying, Mrs. Bauer," 'Betty' asked. "If I hear anything, I could let you know."

"We're at the hotel. Thank you so much."

Carolyn stopped at the stationery store for a notebook, and then made her way to the same high school she and Conrad attended so many years ago. The principal's office listened to her explanation and directed her to two bulletin boards.

43

"Hello, Carolyn," Peter said, as she came through the door.

Conrad's summary of conditions in the house hit her at once.

"Hi, Peter. It's lovely to see you again."

"Conrad's in the kitchen," he said, not bothering to get up from his chair or acknowledging her greeting, which he took to be insincere.

He knew, of course, why she had come, although her sudden appearance seemed odd after the passage of so many years.

Conrad was washing the sink full of dishes.

"Did you find someone?"

She explained about the beauty parlor and high school.

"One of us, or both, will have to wait and see. If I draw a bath, do you think you can talk him into it? He's very unclean, as you explained."

They finished up the dishes together, and Conrad got his brother to agree to a bath. Carolyn found some clean clothes.

"I'll need to do some grocery shopping," Carolyn proposed. "Everything seems under control here at the moment."

"Good. It'll give me a chance to talk to him."

"Are you going to explain to him that it may be necessary to have someone come in regularly?"

"Sure. I'm going to give him all the options and their consequences. But there's something else we need to decide."

"Oh?"

"Yes, would one of the options be his coming to live with us, at least until we can sort things out. Not permanently. But there will be possibilities for indigent care in Sioux City that don't exist here."

"I've been thinking about that, too, Conrad, ever since I arrived and saw his situation firsthand. If you can, find out how he might react to that possibility."

§

"What happened to Carolyn?" Peter asked. "Did she go back home already? Never did like us, did she?"

"No, she's still here. Went shopping. Should be back soon. I don't think she disliked my Griggs relatives.

It's complicated. I'm not sure I understand her feelings. We can talk about it later when we've sorted out these other things."

'Other things' meant Germany and the war. Conrad wanted to talk about it for two reasons. One, to take Peter's mind off his current situation; and two, because he wanted to compare his thoughts to Peter's.

"Changing the subject, I've been wondering, Peter, what you think about the situation in Europe, you know the war that Germany started."

"Germany started? he bristled. "Didn't Britain declare war on Germany?"

"Well, that's debatable. Was that the attitude you took with the FBI?"

"Sort of. I explained that Germany had a right to get out from under the Versailles Treaty. They had every right to rearm."

"Yes, but now Germany has invaded the Soviet Union."

"Bolsheviks! he shouted. "Germany was protecting itself from Bolsheviks!"

"Yeah, but was it smart to invade? That's a huge country. How can Germany control all that? What's more, everything I've read about strategy warns against waging a two-front war. I'm just worried that in time Germany's going to get crushed. Then where *we* will be?"

"Look, Conrad, we've got a president just itching to get into it with Germany. Everybody's after Germany. Hitler saw it coming and decided to hit them first—the French, the British, and now the Russians. I suppose I should say 'Soviets.' Wouldn't surprise me a bit if he hit back at Roosevelt."

"And add another powerful country to put the squeeze on Germany? Kill us and others in the family? That really what you want?"

"No."

"What then?"

"Let him finish of the Bolshies for us!"

"So, the people who reported you to the FBI weren't wrong."

Conrad thought of something else to help him understand his brother.

"Have you ever voted?"

"No, those things had nothing to do with me."

"Why'd you become a citizen, then?"

"Had to. Business licensing, insurance, taxes ... that kind of thing."

"So, you paid taxes."

"Of course. I didn't want the government breathing down my neck, but they came for me anyway, as you saw. I don't know. Maybe we should talk about something else."

"Yeah. So, changing the subject, and I want you to listen to what I have to say and think seriously about it. It seems obvious to Carolyn and me that you can't live alone anymore, and I think you agree with that. You did call out for help, in a way. Remember? There are a couple of options ..."

"Carolyn put up some ads over at the high school for someone to come in, do the cleaning, washing ... even cooking. Basic things. You okay with that?"

"Depends. I'm very tired, Conrad."

"That's fine. Please, close your eyes and try to sleep. I just wanted to make one more suggestion. The other possibility would be for you to live with us *until*, and I stress *until* we find a satisfactory place in town that cares for the elderly. What do you think about that?"

When Peter didn't reply, Conrad looked over and saw he had slumped in his chair.

'Good! He's asleep,' he decided.

44 PREJUDICES

Working as quietly as he could, Conrad continued to clean the kitchen. Fifteen minutes later he thought perhaps Peter would be better off in his bed. He gently touched his brother's arm but got no response. He waited another half minute.

"Peter!" He shook his shoulder.

No response, so, he lifted his wrist to check his pulse. None. He tried Peter's neck, searching for the carotid artery. No luck. But he'd never been able to find a pulse in his own neck or someone else's.

He shook Peter hard. His head lolled back. Conrad now saw that Peter's eyes were open but not blinking. He touched the cornea. No reaction.

He watched Peter's chest for any sign of breathing. He put his ear against the chest but heard nothing.

He found the phone, dialed zero, and told the operator he needed a doctor.

"Is this an emergency," the operator asked.

"Yes, I think my brother has died. He's not breathing and has no pulse"

When she asked, he gave her Peter's address. Ten minutes later an ambulance pulled up outside. Two attendants rushed in with their equipment: stethoscopes, blood pressure sleeves, a bottle of oxygen. They repeated Conrad's checks on Peter and a couple of others before telling Conrad softly that his brother had died.

One of the attendants returned to the ambulance for a cloth stretcher. As they loaded Peter to the stretcher and started for the door, Carolyn burst in, having seen the ambulance outside. Such was her excitement and hurry, she spilled most of the groceries on the front porch.

"Conrad!" she screamed, half in thanks that her husband seemed fine, and half out of concern for the body that lay under a sheet on the stretcher. "What's happened?"

"We were talking, and then we weren't. He just slipped away. Never made a sound. And then Conrad broke down in tears.

Carolyn led him to the divan, sat on the edge next to his hip, and held his hands. The attendants returned to the living room.

"Where are you taking him," Carolyn asked.

"To the morgue. I need a signature that you're releasing the deceased to the morgue."

"He's not the 'deceased,' young man," she said forcefully as she scribbled her name on a paper attached to a clipboard. "His name is *Peter ... Peter Bower*. Are you always so indifferent?"

"I'm very sorry, Ma'am. It's just the way we talk. I wasn't thinking. I meant no disrespect."

Carolyn wanted to pile on about his use of 'Ma'am' as well, but she decided it would detract from the solemnity of the moment, and she would appear to be the unfeeling one.

"Fine. Thank you for explaining," she said softly.

The men left the house and drove away in the ambulance with Peter. Conrad sat up.

"Where are they taking him?"

"To the morgue. I suppose they meant the one at the hospital. I think in the morning we should go over there and make arrangements with a funeral parlor."

"I'm all that's left, besides Philip," he said, shaking his head.

"Please try not to be too down," she implored. "I must pick up the groceries I spilled on the porch. You can help. Keeping busy is important, I think. I'll heat up some Campbell's and make sandwiches, then we should go over to the hotel and get a good night's sleep."

§

Two days later they laid Peter to rest near Marta, William (Billy), and Louise, who had died of heart failure two years earlier. Marta's other son, Philip, attended the services; Ray Clark had remarried and lived in Texas. Julie came with her entire family.

In the days, weeks, and months following Peter's services, Carolyn and Conrad spoke no more of the DAR, shoemakers or coal dealers. Perhaps Peter's sudden death had created some space for reflection. Perhaps it made their running conflict seem small, even petty. Perhaps there was an unspoken feeling that neither could gain anything by continuing old grievances. Life, they had come to know, was short in the hypothetical but a pressing reality at their ages.

Perhaps there was another explanation for their truce. Consider what they buried that day in Griggs. Perhaps the old shoemaker, who had worked hard to serve his community in the only way he knew, who had no Revolutionary ancestor, who was without guile but wrong about Adolf Hitler ... Imagine that the old shoemaker took Carolyn and Conrad's prejudices with him to the grave, prejudices *he* knew were petty and destructive even if *they* hadn't acted on them those many wasted years.

§

Sometime later, a month or two, possibly six months or a year ... the date was not important ... Conrad Bauer placed a call to his daughter. That *was* important. They hadn't spoken since the funeral.

"Hi, Julie."

"Father! Is anything wrong?"

"No, Honey. I just wanted to tell you I went to the library today and checked out their only copy of the works of George Eliot—except the works of George Eliot are not by 'George Eliot.'"

He said it in a way and with a tone of voice that suggested she might not know about Mary Ann Evans, which *he* did. She had tried to put one over on him, he thought, but he was a tad cleverer than she assumed.

Julie had to suppress a laugh; she could tell what he was up to.

"Yes," she replied diplomatically, "but that's another story. Does it matter?"

He didn't reply at once, which raised the sort of internal alarm that children have unconsciously set to alert them when a parent seems unresponsive.

Then ... "I'm going to start *Silas Marner* tonight."

"Goodnight, Daddy."

She had never addressed him so informally. Her heart swelled as she put down the phone.

PART X
AFTERWORD

45   THEN & NOW

This has been a fictionalized account of the improbable union of my paternal grandparents. The truth of its being implausible depended, as you might guess, on my having so little on which to rely: memory, hearsay, documents, witnesses, and ... imagination.

First ... the memories of a small boy: Grandfather was a 'coal dealer,' and my grandmother called my father by a name ('Robert') I'd never heard anyone else use. She commanded a very large kitchen at their home in Davenport, Iowa (right).

Second ... hearsay: According to his niece and nephew, only my grandfather and his carpetbag visited (infrequently) his Ottawa, Illinois ('Griggs, North Dakota'), family.

Third ... the written record: My grandmother was a DAR, and only her signature appeared on the court documents that supported her sons' change of name.

I gleaned more evidence of their lives, most of it circumstantial, from letters and documents found on genealogy websites. Far too much of the story for me as a professional historian required an active imagination and guess work. For example, no one in my family—in my presence—ever uttered a word about Ottawa, great aunts and uncles, or the existence of first and second cousins! But they *were* very real.

The more I struggled to discover this hidden family history the more dissatisfied I became, never able to turn guesses or genealogy into anything approaching certainty. With nowhere else to turn, I decided to visit Ottawa and by prearrangement, meet with two 'cousins.'

§

Fourth ... witnesses. Following a historical conference in Chicago, I drove to Ottawa, a trip of about two hours, to meet with two members of the Fuchs family who turned out to be second cousins. Until I arrived, they had lived, secreted away in a closet belonging to my immediate family; that is, *only* to my father whose silence about Ottawa had been deafening. Whatever my mother knew of the Ottawa family she took to her grave.

A Most Improbable Union 301

My cousins escorted me to the Ottawa Avenue Cemetery. The city of Ottawa is a lovely town situated at the confluence of the Fox and Illinois Rivers. It was a beautiful October day, and the trees boasted to all of Ottawa of their glorious fall foliage.

I listened as we strolled to several embedded stones engraved with the surname 'Fuchs.'

One of the stones read, William F. Fuchs. In my imagination and in this story, it belonged to 'Peter Bauer.'

Not far from William, 'Anna Maria and Louise Bauer' (Maria Barbara and Louisa Fuchs) shared the earth with 'Abigail and Samuel Profit' (Salome Holden and Henry Clay King, one set of maternal great grandparents).

I lingered in Ottawa another day, during which I shared information about my father, his brothers and their families. My astonished cousins had known nothing of 'us,' they said.

§

An additional visit into my familly's past, similar to that of Ottawa—this time on a cross-country bicycle trip—took me to Davenport, Iowa ('Sioux City'). Inside Oakdale Memorial Gardens, a large building housing the final resting place of hundreds, I looked up to the high corner of a nave at two side by side stones,: Gustav F. Fuchs (1870–1951) and Susie K. Fuchs (1869–1957). As a boy, I had known my paternal grandparents only slightly and nothing of their presumed secrets.

§

Fifth ... imagination. I imagined this story in two ways: 1) behind those stones lay 'Conrad' and 'Carolyn Bauer'; and 2) with so little tangible evidence, I had to imagine something of the lives of my 'real' grandparents before inventing 'Conrad' and 'Carolyn.' How did they come to know each other and to marry?

Although Susie Fuchs allowed her sons (Henry, Frederick, and Robert) to change their surname to 'Fox'— quite possibly encouraging them to do so—she never changed hers. I have considered that choice not a legal requirement related to Gustav's coal business, not a convention and not a convenience. I believe it was a quiet, 51-year affirmation of fidelity and love ... But that was just one more guess.

I took fictional liberty—a fancy name for imagination and guesswork—with two related elements of the story, each a different theoretical explanation for 'Carolyn's' late marriage (age 31).

First, the timing of Carolyn's marriage depended on her parents keeping her from men until she was well beyond the age at which young women of that time married.

Second, she wasn't marriageable at all (of scant or of no interest to men)—a 'spinster.'

But consideration of the *timing* of Henry C. King's death and his daughter Susie's marriage led me to dismiss both of those suggestions.

Again, a hypothetical solution to the mystery:

Traditional responsibility of caring for aging parents at that time would have been Susie's, the youngest of Henry and Salome King's four daughters. Consequently, it would have delayed her marrying.

Susie King *did* marry, just fourteen months *after* her father's death and less than a year *before* her mother's! 'Carolyn,' I had to conclude, was neither protected unreasonably nor a spinster. The actual timing of her marriage matched the hypothetical.

§

Photos of family members appear throughout the book.

DEBTS

My principal debt is to a pair of distant cousins in Ottawa, Illinois. My father's cousin, Esther Fuchs Vignali (below right), the daughter of William Fuchs (grandfather's older brother), and Fritz Oppenlander (below center), my grandfather's nephew by marriage *and* my father's cousin. Over two days, they hosted me and opened my eyes to the existence of an extensive but missing part of my family.

My thanks also to my wife, Sheila Ross. It pleases me to say so, although the expression alone does not account for the sum of my gratitude.

As she has for my other books, Sheila read and re-read the manuscript (I'm a frustrating writer for the copy editor; I constantly edit and re-edit) for consistent character behavior, context, grammar, and spelling.

Wikipedia provided information on subjects beyond my familiarity: steerage; the DAR; the Homestead and Pacific Railway Acts; the Northern Pacific Railroad; the evolution of 'Dakota'; pump manufacturing and mechanics; shoemaking (including guild requirements); coal deliveries; Bauhaus design; the development of Sioux City; the S.S. *Stuttgart*; and so forth.

Any grammatical errors or spelling mistakes are my responsibility.

AUTHOR

Stephen Carey Fox is a Navy veteran of the Vietnam Era and Emeritus Professor of American History at Humboldt State University (now Cal Poly Humboldt) where his teaching career spanned four decades.

Steve is the author of award-winning articles and book-length oral/documentary histories of the relocation and internment of Europeans of enemy nationality in the United States during World War II.

In retirement, he turned to writing fiction for the pleasure of 'telling lies for fun.' His books consider crime, history, feminism, reminiscence, family and contemporary political, economic and social issues.

Steve writes from behind northern California's 'Redwood Curtain' in Willow Creek, a village renowned as the home of Sasquatch (a.k.a. Bigfoot) and 'medicinal gardens.'

Made in the USA
Columbia, SC
11 August 2024